CAYCE-WEST COLUMBIA LIBRARY

9502 9100 228 766 0

New
2-10-16

FIC GUS

Gussow, Adam.
Busker's Holiday

D0887811

CAYCE-WEST COLUMBIA
BRANCH LIBRARY
1500 AUGUSTA ROAD
WEST COLUMBIA, S. C. 29169

BUSKER'S HOLIDAY

ADAM GUSSOW

MODERN BLUES HARMONICA

Busker's Holiday

© 2015 Adam Gussow

All rights reserved. This book or any portion thereof may not be reproduced or used in any manner whatsoever without the express written permission of the publisher except for the use of brief quotations in a book review.

Published by Modern Blues Harmonica

ISBN: 978-0-99671-240-8

for Peter Herman

Paris Blues

P aris is where the madness starts, that summer of my plunge into the busking life. I've fled the wreckage of the bittersweet almost-marriage I shared with Helen Solomon for five long years in New York. Her most recent fling has led her to move out of our third and final apartment. My last-minute travel partner is Paul Goldberg, a fellow English Ph.D. candidate at Columbia. A bearded Jewish Montrealer with his own insecurities, he has a bracing sense of life as something nasty, brutish, and short but also capable of being survived and savored. He's a Renaissance scholar, which may prove useful. I'm newly womanless, in need of rebirth. At twenty-six, my old life is gone. Done. But I have a plan.

I used to be a freelance literary journalist. That was my extra-curricular ambition: to fuse Hemingway's compression with Kerouac's dynamism in a distinctly contemporary critical voice. I am now a blues harmonica player. This is what I know how to do and *have* known how to do since the moment when my only other real girl-friend left me for a stringy-haired guitar player back in high school. The street-performance angle is an innovation, though. The idea of working my blues out before a foreign public is new and compel-ling. I have five weeks to burn through Europe, a heart fanged by hellhounds, and a battery-powered amp: a Mouse that roars. I also have two journals: a hundred and sixty blank pages that I'm determined to fill. Summer romance, Dionysian excess. Anything to keep my mind off the sex Helen is having back in America with a guy who is not me.

The open road was the last place I expected to end up with Paul Goldberg. We'd met in the fall of my second year in the program, a late 1980s moment when the Reagan years were winding down and everything was falling apart. This was back in the dark ages before iPhones and selfies, before Facebook and YouTube and blogs and "friending," when people shared ideas and feelings face-to-face, rather than on screens, and sometimes actually became friends. Paul was the guy with thinning hair and teardrop glasses who kept raising his hand in Renaissance Poetry, volunteering obscure tidbits about poets and poetic trends. Lorenzo Fiorella da who? Risorgimento da what? He didn't just know his stuff, he showboated his knowingness. The guy bothered me.

One day he quoted Saul Bellow to support a point about Puritan attacks on the troubadours. I'd written my senior thesis at Cornell on The Fool's Romantic Quest in *Henderson the Rain King*. I hadn't gone near Bellow since then—I'd turned into a Hemingway–Kerouac specialist—but I still retained exclusive quoting rights, or imagined I did. I raised my hand and insisted that Bellow's conception of the absurd hero wasn't *really* the same as Sydney's conception of the lyric poet because blah blah blah blah blah.

It was like jabbing a hermit crab with a stun gun. He swelled up and glared, then counterattacked with an icy observation about *The Dean's December*, which I'd gotten as a gift, read partway into, and shelved. Grad school was brutal: admit ignorance and you were toast. I started to bluff when Alice Blankenship—a small, smooth-faced woman from Connecticut who wore grey cashmere and pearls and kept interrupting her lectures to remark that if we thought Columbia-out-of-South-Africa protestors shouting through bullhorns below our classroom window were something, we should have been around back in the sixties when the SDS took over Hamilton Hall, they really knew how to get things done—gave us a look and said, "Let's move on, shall we?" We slouched and eyed each other.

I hooked my cowboy jacket off my chair after the bell rang and drifted toward him.

He was cleaning his glasses—baring his teeth as he fogged them, polishing them on his *Merry Wives of Windsor* sweatshirt. He smiled awkwardly; my heart softened. I put out my hand and said it was nice to meet somebody who liked Bellow, it seemed like everybody in the department was into deconstruction or—

"I *hate* deconstruction," he barked, slipping on his glasses.

For the next five minutes he lectured me on the sins of Derridians, Foucauldians, and all others who dared claim that a text meant anything other than precisely what its author intended. What was poetry if not the spontaneous, directed, and willful overflow of powerful emotion? Throw out the singer and you might as well kiss the song goodbye. All such erasures being, of course, a symptom of the West's general decadence. A purple dinosaur named Barney—I love you, you love me—being the counterexample that proved his point.

He flailed away for a while, then trailed off.

"Anyway," I murmured. We were avoiding each other's eyes. I stuck out my hand. "Your name's Paul, isn't it?"

"Goldberg with a G."

"McKay Chernoff. Yeah, Blankenship keeps going 'Yes, Paul' whenever you raise your hand, so I figured."

"Terrific. I've made a nuisance of myself already."

"It's impressive as shit, man. I'm seriously depressed."

He shrugged. "I love the material, I read everything I can get my hands on, I live an incredibly boring life."

"What are you, writing your dissertation on the stuff?"

"Master's essay, actually."

"You're only a first-year?"

He gave me a dry look. "That would be the implication."

A bell rang down below.

"I hate to be rude," I said, hoisting my daypack, "but I gotta take a piss and head on over to Ferris Booth to meet my girlfriend. You mind if we, ah…?"

He gestured toward the men's room door. "After you."

I shouldered through and slid in front of the lone urinal. He thumped into the stall to my left. The window was open; it was a breezy fall day. Protestors were chanting rhythmically in the plaza below. Paul gushed merrily away.

"So where you from?" I asked, staring at the chrome-plated flush mechanism.

"Montreal."

"Canadian?"

"Born and bred, hey."

"I could have sworn you were from New York."

"Cote St.-Luc. The Jewish quarter."

"Parlez-vous francais?"

"Un peu."

"Moi aussi. Especialment avec les beautiful jeunes filles."

I zipped my fly and flushed, then reached into my hip pocket and pulled out a harp. Paul was banging around inside his stall.

"Yo, check it out." I wailed on the Four Hole, then slid all the way up and screamed on the bent Ten Hole.

There was a moment of echoey silence followed by a thunderous flush. Paul came out of the stall. "What *are* you doing?"

I flapped my cupped hands. "Whammer Jammer, lemme hear ya, Dickie!"

"Magic Dick." He pronounced the name slowly, voluptuously, like the label on a bottle of twenty-year old Scotch.

"You know about those guys?"

"I was a nice repressed Jewish boy, J. Geils was a nice Jewish boy acting out his wildest and most decadent fantasies, my mother had a nervous breakdown every time she heard the stuff."

"J. Geils was Jewish?"

"The whole band was: Peter Wolf, Seth Justman, the bearded little troll who played bass...."

"Danny Klein."

He gave me a smug grin. "Nice Jewish boys."

I stared at him. Bearded chipmunk-cheeks, hands shoved in back pockets. The pedant in action.

"We gotta get out of here," I said, "or my girlfriend's gonna kill me."

His grin tightened. "I should be so lucky."

"Tell me about it."

"On second thought, celibacy has its advantages."

I veered sideways through the fire door. "You'll meet Helen one of these days."

"So invite me along."

I swung around the banister and down the next flight. "We're sort of getting over a little fight."

"She's raking you over the coals."

"You have no idea."

"Someday I'll tell you about Judith and you'll know just how wrong you are."

We bounced into the front lobby. Light was flooding through the windows onto the grey tile floor. Specks of dust spun and shimmered in the dead air.

"Yeah well," I muttered. "At least it's a nice day outside."

"I'll remember that while I'm burrowing through the stacks."

We pushed through the front doors and squinted into the hazy sun. The air smelled heavy and green, like grass waiting to be mowed. I stuck out my hand. "The wife awaits."

"The wyf awaiteth."

"Thanks for putting up with my little outburst."

He let go and saluted stiffly. "You go have your romantic lunch, I'll go run my boring errands, I'll see you…."

"Thursday in class."

"Right."

He pivoted and marched off. He had a funny way of walking—tilted forward on the balls of his feet, like he was chasing something, or fleeing.

He knew quite a lot about blues, it turned out. We became friends. He was a good guy to have around that fall and winter. My life was a mess, although I couldn't quite see it. Mining my own despair, confronting apocalypse with tautly controlled prose, I'd had a productive year, writing a pair of essays—one on Hemingway's wartime infidelities, another on Kerouac's stylistic velocity in the context of postwar nuclear anxieties—that had been snapped up by the quarterlies and slated for summer publication. As Helen slowly drifted away, I burrowed deeper. But my heart was aching. Sometimes, walking up Broadway to campus, I'd cut through the service tunnel just past 120th Street, pull out my harp, and wail as I passed the guard booth, hoping that the security guard, *anybody*, would hear the pain. Spring, with all its hormone-driven yearnings, just made things worse. We were having cappuccino at Ferris Booth Cafe one rainy afternoon in April; I was raving about Helen. He finally put up his hands after I'd been groaning for half an hour about our latest miserable fight.

"May I make a suggestion?"

"Kick her out?"

"First thing tomorrow morning."

"Nah," I said, waving my hand, "that's too easy. She *wants* me to tell her to get the fuck out instead of growing up and realizing she can't have everything, she can't keep stringing me and that other asshole along and breaking my goddamn heart every time she turns around. At some point she's gonna get so disgusted she's gonna *have* to move out because she won't be able to live with herself if she doesn't." I tossed back the last of my cappuccino.

He shrugged. "So much for suggestions."

"I mean I've obviously *thought* about kicking her out, I just can't bring myself to...to...I mean if I just stick with her a little longer and show her how much I really *do* care about making the relationship work maybe she'll...she'll...ah fuck. I don't know."

"Forget it."

I shook my head. "I probably should have kicked her out a long time ago."

He said nothing. I rubbed the back of my neck, stared out the window at the wet grey day. Little buds were beginning to sprout on the bushes next to the patio. A young woman in a poncho was pushing a stroller up the college walk. The kid in the stroller was wearing a bright yellow rain suit and flapping his arms. Laughing, blowing spit-bubbles.

I sighed. "The last thing I feel like doing is heading over to the library."

Paul was cleaning his glasses. "I actually have an errand to run over at the Student Travel Agency before I head back." He slipped them on. "Do you have any idea how much it costs to fly to Paris these days?"

"Five hundred rountrip?"

"Try six-fifty-four, not to mention that those are American dollars which are thirty percent more expensive than Canadian."

"Bummer."

"I'm still trying to figure out how I'm supposed to finance a month over there without ending up homeless when I get back."

"Whoa whoa whoa—you're what?"

"Didn't I tell you?"

"I think I would have remembered a trivial little detail like you abandoning me."

He looked stung. "I had no idea I was required to submit my vacation plans for prior approval."

"It's not a question of submitting your...ah Christ, forget it."

"We seem a little testy today."

"So you're going on vacation," I said, lacing my arms across my chest.

"Leave early June, return early July."

"The mini-Grand Tour."

He shrugged. "I was hoping to hit Paris before the tourist-swarms descend."

I leaned back, sighing. "The only time I've ever been to Paris was five years ago and the whole point was making sure Helen didn't sleep with other guys."

He rolled his eyes. "Were you *born* a masochist?"

"Nah, she was over there on a Fulbright—I was finishing up my senior year at Cornell and I missed her so badly I figured if I don't put in a personal appearance at least once in nine months she's gone. So I flew over for Christmas." I shook my head. "Turned out she'd been screwing some Scottish guy from the Sorbonne, which made things fifty times more intense. It was a great trip in the sense that if I *hadn't* gone she probably would have left me, instead of coming back to New York after I graduated and moving in with me."

"And making your life hell for the next five years."

I tilted my cup on the saucer, stared at the last few drops of spiderwebby brown scum. The tables around us were bustling with the four o'clock crowd. We glanced at each other. Paul smoothed his flyaway hair. "Shall we?"

"The salt mines await," I sighed.

Paul reached for his collapsible umbrella as we stood up. "Just out of curiosity, what are your plans for the summer?"

I heaved my daypack. "Write a couple of essays, run a couple of races. Fight with the wife."

"So come along already."

I stared. "With you?"

"You'd still have most of the summer to do whatever you wanted back here."

"I mean it's a wild idea, I'm just—"

"You're afraid the wife will say no."

"Nah, I'm just—"

"Ah, you're afraid she'll say, 'Fine, go right ahead.'"

"Fuck. I mean if I head over there with you and leave her alone in New York that's *it*. You know? She'll be jumping Lonnie's bones the moment I set foot on the plane."

"Look," he said, "these things don't need to be decided right now. You may wake up tomorrow morning and feel differently, Helen may decide to mend her evil ways."

"Lonnie may get blown to pieces by a trip-wired terrorist down in Times Square."

We were chuckling grimly as we pushed into the front lobby. The door of the Student Travel Agency was propped open; I could see a faded poster of whitewashed brick houses rising above a gorgeous deep-blue bay with a caption reading "Beirut: Jewel of the Middle East."

Paul raised his hand like somebody being sworn in. "You go bury yourself in the library, I'll blow my life savings on a ticket to paradise, I'll see you...."

"At the funeral."

"Get some sleep," he sighed.

We grabbed hands and shook. I spun and shouldered through the front door.

The rain had stopped. Everything outside was heavy, wet, green. Lots of earthy fragrances pushing out of bud-covered shrubs. Pachysandra, forsythia. I paused and took a couple of deep breaths. For a moment I almost felt like crying. Spring is here! Awake, arise, or be forever fallen! Then the feeling faded. I heaved my daypack onto my shoulder and headed towards the library, head down.

You were standing in the baggage-claim area waiting for your suitcase to come around, dazed by the overnight flight from New York, when you heard her call out. Everything after that was a blur: you were turning, she was grinning and waving, you had a second to get ready and then she was throwing herself into your arms and you were hugging her, rubbing your cheek against hers and pulling back to look—she was so much more *real* than the snapshots you'd been hoarding all fall, she was your sweet, silly animal and you were kissing the fine black fur at her temples, she was gazing cross-eyed at your mouth as you leaned forward, your heart was suddenly aching because her lips were so much softer than you'd remembered, the musky smell of her breath made all the difference.

The ride back to her place on the Metro was a dreamy blur. How could you be holding her hand in Paris this morning when only last night you'd been sitting at the gate in JFK trying desperately to remember what she looked like? You were under her wing now; she was taking you to the girls' school where she'd been living and teaching since September. When you thought about making love for the first time in four months your heart felt impossibly light and sweet. Stations slid by, doors hissed open and shut. She kept lifting your hand to her lips. Another half hour you'd be home, wherever that was. Ten minutes after that you'd be together.

The train slid to a stop. She muscled your suitcase onto the platform like the crew jock she'd been only a year before. The Auberge des Etudiennes was halfway between Raneleigh and Jasmin; the throaty way she pronounced both stations gave you a thrill. Her Chanel perfume, her loosely-knotted silk scarves. How could so worldly a woman be so in love with a guy like you? Twenty-two to your twenty. She hauled your suitcase up the steps, out into the cold clear December morning. The sun was shining, doors of little shops were tinkling open and shut. You made her stop in front of a patisserie at block's end while you feasted your eyes: eclairs, petit fours, chaussons aux pommes. You grinned and shook your head. So this was Paris, huh? You'd definitely come back and check this place out. You slung your arm around her neck and gave her a big sloppy kiss. The moment your tongues touched, her body stiffened; her eyes were swimming when you pulled away. You made a face and panted; she giggled. Four months hadn't changed *that*.

You took turns lugging your suitcase back to the Auberge. Rounding a corner and there it was: fifty agonized letters you'd hurled at these gates, those walls. Dozens of teenaged girls were calling out to each other as they flooded down the front steps; two days before Christmas, everybody rushing to make connections home. Most of them chirped "Goodbye Miss Solomon," several flashed you embarrassed smiles. She grinned and rubbed your back as you heaved yourself up the steps. She couldn't wait to show you the apartment you'd be sharing. The courtyard, the kitchenette, the queen-sized bed. She'd made special arrangements with the Auberge because her studio was too small for the two of you.

You were pushing through the front door when a dark-haired girl swung to a stop, took your hand and began chattering. Her name was Marianna Baaziz, she was wonderfully happy to meet you. She was at this moment making great haste to catch a train for Cologne or she would have been most delighted to stop and chat. She kissed you three times on each cheek. "Bye bye! Tchuss! Au revoir!" German-Algerian, you learned as you were kicking your suitcase onto the elevator. That's why they'd become friends: both were half-somethings, neither fit in here the way the French girls did.

Then the elevator doors were opening and you were pushing your suitcase down the hall as your Hawaiian-eyed goddess trotted ahead. You stared at her ass—remembering, suddenly, how hot she looked lying face down on her bed with nothing on but blue silk panties. The softness of her belly when she rolled over, the feel of her large brown nipples hardening under your tongue.

She stuck her key in a doorknob and pushed—a flash of sunlight—and you followed her in. You set down your suitcase, she slipped an arm around your waist. What did you think? She ran her hand back through her hair. The white bowl of oranges in the middle of the living room table was the first thing you noticed. Japanese print on one wall, Matisse's maenads whirling across the other. She steered you into the kitchen to show you the refrigerator stocked with wine and brie, back through the living room into the bedroom. A pot of brilliant red carnations next to the bed, a Charlie-Brown sized Christmas tree next to the window.

What did you think? You put your mouth against her forehead and stood silently, lost in the smooth warm touch of her skin. Her temple was next, then the side of her face. You spent a long time on the side of her face. For some reason you couldn't stop kissing the side of her face. Lots of little kisses. Thousands of tiny kisses with your hand stroking her hair. By the time your lips found hers she was no more than a wet salty blur, fingers shivering into your thigh.

I t's raining in Paris on the morning Paul and I arrive, dizzy from the long sleepless flight. Our introduction to French civilization is a five-floor pensione with no elevator commanded by a gypsy-turbaned matron who eyes my Mouse with suspicion. Paul and I visit the Louvre with his friend Liz, a bitchy bosomy former classmate at McGill who works for the *International Herald Tribune* and is the welcoming mat he's arranged. We gaze at Mona Lisa through a greenish protective shield; I can barely see the smile. Later we order *croque monsieurs* and *vin rouge* in a crowded brasserie in the Latin Quarter. Paul and Liz seem to be reconnecting; I don't think they were an item, but I'm not sure. I head back to the pensione early through the swirling mist, cringe through the foyer under the gypsy woman's gaze, write a few words in my first journal, and cry briefly before falling asleep.

Paul's backpack is lying open on his untouched bed when I awake. I leap out of my own bed, pad over to the window of our pensione, and push the curtains back. The courtyard is a rat's nest of clotheslines stretched between crumbling brick walls and balloon-tired bicycles tangled in a corner. The sky—what little I can see—is promising. A sapphire-blue trapezoid, taut as a drumhead. Streaks of sun glinting off upper windows across the way. I take a deep shivering breath, jerk my head inside and grab a towel off the dresser.

I pull on jeans and a fresh t-shirt when I get back from the shower—KEROUAC: THE MOVIE is skunky from the plane ride over, so I go with JUST DO IT—and then I upend my daypack and take stock. Fifteen Hohner Marine Band harps, G through F# plus spares. The scratched grey Shure mike I used with the Snakedrivers back in Ithaca. A Boss digital delay footpedal for that wailing-in-the-bathroom sound. A Swiss Army knife with corkscrew to facilitate emergency red wine. The Panama hat purchased at a Korean-owned novelty stand in midtown Manhattan forty-eight hours ago. I glance over at the bidet: one out-of-the-box Mouse, juiced. I yank out the charge-cord and heave it onto my bed. Angled black mesh veiling the speaker cone, trapezoidal black sides trimmed with chrome. I snatch up a harp and dance around the room, yowling into my cupped hands. B-flat is a sweet key: a half-notch more tautly-sprung than A, like an alloy tennis racket after wood.

I clap harps into boxes and clatter them into my daypack, then flip open my journal, scrawl a note for Paul, and put it on his pillow. First bottle tonight is on me. I hook my Mouse off the bed, slap on my Panama, and head out.

Damp cobblestones are drying in the sun as I swing down through the Latin Quarter, breezes tickling my bare arms. The shadowed air next to the souvlaki shops has the cool sweet smell of a flawless June day about to unfold. I pause to stare through the window of Patisserie du Sud Tunisien at trays of filo-dough pastries oozing honey, then cut around the corner to Boulevard Saint Michel. Cafe au Saint Severin is bustling; I kick my Mouse under a front-row table. I've been to this city before and know what I want: croissants avec beurre et confitures and enough freshly-blended café creme to vaporize all remaining traces of chickenshit.

I give the aproned waiter my order and kick back. A couple of Hell's Angels in scuffed black leather are slumped against Harleys next to the marble fountain across the street. The boulevard is a flurry of moussed young men in pinstripes kissing their fingers as they bump shoulders with young women in wasp-waist jeans and t-shirts reading BROOKLYN BIG-TIME SURF CHAMP and PARIS, TEXAS: UNLIMITED RUGGEDNESS. Every tautly-stretched piece of fabric seems to outline another set of jiggling nipples. Not just young women: fifty-year-old Catherine Deneuves with pillowed lips and tossed hair. Curves like the hulls of a thousand racing yachts. They started all that. Hungry, starving, I reach down between my legs for my journal.

The waiter is back with a wicker basket of croissants, little dishes of butter and jam, a white china pot of steamed milk and large cup half-filled with espresso. I pour, stir, chug, wolf. Everything tightens into sharp hot focus. I flip open my journal and begin listing the songs I used to sing with the Snakedrivers. Rattlesnake moans, evil-gal laments. I go back through and cross off everything I'm not going to have the nerve to sing a capella through a battery-powered amp in the middle of the Beaubourg plaza. I take another hit of creme. Maybe I need to get drunk. Maybe I need to buy a large bottle of red wine. Maybe that will help me sing like B. B. King instead of a broken-hearted white boy.

By the time I stand up, shafts of sunlight are cutting through the chestnut trees overhead. I teeter in front of my empty cup and scan the revised lineup:

Good Morning Blues
Sweet Home Chicago
Take You Downtown
You Ain't Nothin' But a Hound Dawg
Baby Please Don't Go
Poor Boy Blues
Driftin' Blues
Every Day I Have the Blues
Traintime
Key to the Highway
Southbound

Every tune can be played as an instrumental; I don't have to sing. Just milk my blue-notes for that Sonny Boy sob, scream like Magic Dick on the upper holes. Keep things moving until money starts pouring in. The plan is simple: open up a vein and bleed for spare change. At least I'm not dying a slow death back in New York, alone in my big empty bed.

Half an hour later I'm sitting on my upended Mouse at the top of the Beaubourg plaza, picking at an early lunch—ham-and-brie-on-a-baguette and a cup of FastBurger red wine—and trying to ignore the stench of stale urine rising from massive ventilator shafts on either side of me. People are scattered across the cobblestones down below: gazing up at the red and blue ventilator pipes, consulting guide-books, snapping photographs. Caricature artists are lounging beside portable easels near the front doors. A tribe of blond hippies is dozing near the top of the slope: smudged backpacks, Icelandic sweaters, empty wine bottles. An Asian guy in a cowboy hat is strumming and singing Eagles songs to a small crowd, crooning Well I'm aaaaaaaaalready gone.

I wolf down my crusts, drain the last few drops and stand up. No way am I playing without beer. I scan, then lurch across the walkway, pull out a couple of ten-franc coins and buy a pair of lime-green Heinekens from a young black guy with dreadlocks working a kiosk. I unzip my daypack and shove one down into the tangle of electrical cables, zip up and sling it over my shoulder, crack open the other can and take a long gulping suck. I belch quietly. Nobody in Paris knows who I am. A hundred years from now I'll be rotting in my grave.

I kill my beer and walk down along the sloping edge of the plaza with the concrete wall rising next to me, sun beating on my hat. I set my Mouse in the shade by the wall, crouch and unzip, pulling out my mike and footpedal, the second can of Heineken and my journal plus four or five harps. When everything is plugged in I grab the daypack and zip both sides halfway up, arranging it a couple of feet in front of my Mouse. Dig into my pocket, toss a few coins, then turn and float towards my rig. I twirl down the volume and pick up the mike. Flip open my journal. I glance at the second can of Heineken, then grab it, rip it, and take a long bracing blast. The hippies are sprawled in the shade, hair matted, out of it. I palm a harp. Blow a couple of test notes into the mike. Volume low and unobtrusive, sound echoey and plaintive. There remains the small question of playing the first note. There remains the small question of just oh for chrissake will you just stop fucking *worrying* about it you chickenshit wimp-ass goddamn—

Then I leap out of the plane. My bodyweight evaporates; the world is a vast cobblestoned void into which I've been thrown with a microphone and harmonica gripped between chilled hands. There are pilgrims wandering past who might make me an offering. Several pause, then move on. I'm pushing too hard. My shuffle rhythms are jerky. There's a sickening weight on my heart. I'm alone in the middle of a vast sunlit waste.

After ten minutes, trembling, I pull the mike away and crouch down. Three or four people have given me money. I've probably got enough to buy another Heineken.

"Hey."

I glance up to see a skinny longhaired guy bouncing towards me with a guitar case and a small Fender amp. He looks like a painter hauling paint, shoulders sloping. Freckles, a pug nose, very pale.

"You finished?" he says as he sets down his stuff.

I rub the back of my neck. "The spot's yours, man."

"You're from the States?"

"New York."

"New York? That's brilliant." He sticks out a hand. "London."

"Seriously, man, I'm through."

"New York," he muses, pulling a pack of Marlboros out of his breast pocket. "Busking's a bit better back home, I suppose?"

"I've ah...seen a lot of jazz guys playing down by Columbus Circle." I'm staring at his guitar-case plastered with stickers for Antibes, Geneva, the Bulldog Cafe in Amsterdam. "What kind of stuff you into?"

He blows a cloud of smoke. "Blues, jazz. Beatles tunes for the tourists. The usual shit."

"Blues?"

"I'm not much of a lead player." He smiles. His teeth are bad. "Don't suppose you'd want to team up? My name's Finney, by the way."

"McKay." I'm grinning as we slap. "Hell yeah."

"Brilliant. Now what we've gotta do...." He glances over his shoulder. "The best pitch is down front, between those two pipes."

I follow his line of sight. Bottom of the plaza, with the building looming behind us.

"We're not gonna get in trouble down there?"

He takes a last sizzling hit, blows smoke out the side of his mouth as he flicks his butt. "By the time the flics show up we'll be sitting at the pub round back getting trashed."

"Flics?"

"Cops." He picks up his guitar and amp, one in each hand. "I wouldn't worry about them. It's the fucking CRS you've got to watch out for."

"The CRS?"

"Military police." He jerks his chin. "Need a hand?"

"No, I'm fine." I crouch and start clapping harps into boxes.

"I'll stitch up the spot." He bounces off.

I pack up, grab my Mouse and swing down across the plaza. The Beaubourg looms like the glittery silicon innards of an Earth-devouring mainframe coiled by ribbed lucite Anacondas. Finney is sitting on his amp cradling his cream-colored Strat, guitar case open. I hook up while he smokes. The Asian cowboy is crooning inanely just above us. I toot my A-harp; Finney twangs, fiddles with the tuning peg, then shushes me and finishes up.

"Ready or not." He rakes the strings. His amp barks.

"You think we oughta start off that loud?"

"It's the only way, really. You've got to bash people over the head or they'll walk right by."

I grin. "You're a maniac, man."

"Be a shit-lousy busker if I wasn't."

I crouch next to my Mouse, dial up the volume, and honk. Notes ricochet off the plate glass at our backs.

Finney chuckles. "Buckle up." Then he slams into a straight-four strum: chunk chunka chunk chunk. The beat is there, it's shaky at first and then I ease into the groove, hit a few fat notes, and we're swinging.

Within thirty seconds there are five or six hippies sprawled at our feet and a dozen more staggering down. A couple toss change into Finney's case before collapsing; the rest kick back, pull out packages of Drum tobacco and start rolling cigarettes, heads bobbing. Sleeping bags are unfurled, bottles of wine emerge. Finney's tight funky rhythm makes my harp sound jazzy and huge. As we dig down into the groove, a bare-chested guy in stained lederhosen spirals in and starts dancing. He has knotty brown legs, muttonchop whiskers with a ferocious underbite: an officer from the Prussian army on a back-to-nature kick. He cycles through a series of bodybuilding poses before swinging to a stop—grinning wolfishly, hands outstretched. Taps his head, nods at my hat. I pull it off. He whirls around and dips low. Almost everybody tosses a coin or two; people in back horseshoe what they have. He pirouettes toward us and holds out the hat like a maitre d' in a fancy restaurant brandishing a freshly-broiled filet mignon. We've fucking *killed*. He kneels, emptying it with a flourish into Finney's case, a river of coins.

I've just taken the hat back and slapped it on when Finney stops strumming and the music dies.

"What's up?" I pant.

He's crouching and unplugging. "Time to go."

I turn to discover a large well-groomed man standing behind me. Grey tweed jacket, maroon pullover sweater, mustache. His lips are moving. He is addressing me in witheringly precise French. He's outraged. Scandalized! He begins to list the diverse bestialities I have perpetrated on the French government, the city of Paris, and the glorious institution in whose tenebrous shadow I have committed such a reprehensible act of criminal mischief. He lifts his arm towards the top of the plaza. Have I not seen the sign? *Les amplificateurs sont interdites.*

I look into the distance. Next to the piss-smelling ventilator shafts. Sont interdites. Are forbidden.

He lowers his arm. If I or my vagabond accomplice are ever again seen engaging in such criminally mischievous activities on the grounds of the Centre National D'Art et De Culture Georges Pompidou he will see to it personally that his security forces are given strict instructions to confiscate our equipment and deliver us to the local prefect of police. Is this clear?

"Oui monsieur," I murmur. The word *confisquer* is luminous.

"Bon." He shoots his cuffs and strides away.

I stand paralyzed. Kids at the back of the crowd hoot and give him the finger, others salute me with wine bottles and spiral out across the plaza. Everybody else piles forward. Money flutters and clinks into Finney's case from a dozen directions; people want to know my name, where I'm from. Girls jostle each other and flirt. Finney pushes through after a moment and throws an arm around my neck.

"That was brilliant. I've never seen anybody handle him like that."

I don't know whether to hug the guy or kill him. "You're too fucking much, man."

He shows his bad teeth. "Of course I am."

The muttonchopped dancer swings around the side of our mob and claps Finney's shoulder. "It goes okay now," he says breathlessly.

Finney smiles vaguely. "Hey man."

The dancer puts out his hand. "Je m'appelle Jorg."

"McKay," I say. He has a strong grip.

"Ta musique, c'est super."

"Merci."

He's leaning on Finney's shoulder, legs crossed. He shakes his mane. "Alors, on va partager maintenant?"

Finney glances at the change, blows smoke skyward. "How much you want?"

A lazy, wolfish smile.

Finney eyes him warily, then hooks the larger man's neck in a playful choke. Jorg bursts out laughing.

A harmonica hoots just behind me. A young guy in top-hat and tails is gazing at me, hands cupped. Dark eyes, hooked nose, curly black hair, a gold stud in one earlobe. He palms a flattened, rusted harp. "I like this way you were playing. It is too bad this asshole flies out of his cave to tell you—" He makes a cut sign across his throat, frowning.

I glance at the tangled mess at my feet. "I better clean up this shit before he comes back and throws me in jail."

He snorts. "Fucking asshole shit."

"You wanna hang out and trade licks? I'll buy you a beer."

"Licks? I have no licks." He cups his harp, dark eyes blazing, and lets out a loud Whooooooaugh!

"Hey, check it out." I grab my harp and nail the bent Ten Hole with wild vibrato.

Suddenly he's smiling. "Where do you learn these notes?"

"Magic Dick, the J. Geils Band."

"Give me a hand before this Nazi bastard does!" Finney shouts, crouching next to his guitar case. Jorg is hovering.

"Hang on," I holler, zipping up. The harp player touches my arm.

"Tonight. Twenty hours. I will meet with you at Le Mazet."

"I'm not real up on the Metro stops."

"No no, Le Mazet is a bar where everybody in Paris goes to get shitnosed when they finish playing the cafes. Finney can show you."

He leans in, backhanding his mouth. "We will drink beer and watch the pretty girls and you will explain me all your licks of magical dick."

"Now you're talking."

"Good." He clears his throat roughly, like a smoker. "I must go now and draw ugly pictures that make people look like giraffes and hyenas."

He darts across the cobblestones, coattails flying. As he disappears into the Beaubourg I suddenly realize that he's never told me his name.

I'm journaling in bed next morning, hand cramping, when Paul knocks and sticks his head through the door. His hair is bristling away from his receding hairline. He's gazing at me over the rims of his teardrop-shaped glasses.

"Knock knock," he says dryly.

"Hey, long time no see." I sit up and swat my hair. "Did you get my note last night?"

He shuts the door. "I couldn't *read* your note last night."

"Meet me at Le Mazet on Rue St. Andre des Arts?"

He glares silently. Eloquently.

"Shit. You got my note yesterday morning, though?"

"Those hieroglyphs I did manage to translate."

I shake my head. "This is turning into a bizarre little vacation."

"You said it, I didn't."

I fall back in bed. My head is not in great shape. "You won't believe the day I had."

"I'm afraid to ask."

Suddenly I'm raving, spewing sheets of sound. Rocking the Beaubourg with Finney! Spare change streaming into his guitar case! Grabbing our amps and smoking a back-alley joint, floating across

Boulevard de Sebastopol into Chatelet/Les Halles down three flights of escalators, hooking up with Jackson—big-bellied irritable scar-faced drummer from Cameroon—and running off a string of songs with the trains whooshing by until French cops swoop down, unplugging and dividing the drumcase full of money two Italian girls have collected—Jackson wants to play another set after the flics split, he keeps patting the air barking *Reposer un peu!* until Finney gives him the finger and we split, fly back up three flights and burst into the sunny afternoon, kick our amps under a café table next to a fountain, flop into plastic wicker chairs and order Cokes. Thick old-fashioned Coke bottles with red-and-white logos scuffed from thousands of refillings, the first two so icy with feathered crystals that we order another pair and a third. We kick back and drink, Finney smokes and talks—he dropped out of art school in London last fall, hitchhiked to Amsterdam before Paris—and when I look at my watch it's almost six-thirty, time to touch base with Paul at the pensione. We stand up with hip pockets sagging, pay our tab with handfuls of change and head toward the Latin Quarter. The Seine is shimmering when we reach the far side of the Ile de la Cité; Finney stops to smoke another cigarette while I lean against the bridge with the breeze ruffling my shirtsleeves and inhale the river down below, Notre Dame Cathedral up ahead, Latin Quarter on my right, grey fortress on my left. I'm in the game.

Then we hike the last leg to the pensione, I drop off my Mouse, scrawl the note for Paul, and we're back on the street. Le Mazet is buskers lounging around tables, kicked back in chairs with acoustic guitars and harp racks shouting "Sympathy for the Devil," a cellist with his stringy-haired girlfriend counting a coconut-mound of change in back. Matteo—the caricature artist—shows up and I empty my pockets for beers and more beers. Finney drifts away for a while, then floats back in, hauls his guitar and Porta-Champ out from under the pinball machine and says meet him at two-thirty this afternoon in front of Chatelet without my Mouse so we can work the trains before hitting the Beaubourg. We bump shoulders and he's gone. Matteo and I lean against a car out front and trade licks, drink beer, trade harps; by the end of the night he has me hooting like Sonny Terry and flirting with every pretty girl who walks by—"oppressing them with my patriarchal gaze," as Ms. Super Feminist would call it. *Fuck* Helen! Fuck her and Lonnie and that whole goddamned snake pit of an English department. *This* is living. That bullshit is behind me.

Paul is scratching his beard when I finish. He sighs. "I take a vacation, I'm thankful if I see a couple of memorable paintings and avoid contracting amoebic dysentery."

"It's gonna be twice as good today. Finney told me about some festival of street musicians they're having where the flics have to lay low because it's an official holiday. Plus it's a Saturday. We're gonna clean *up*, man." I toss my journal aside and pad across the floor to check the recharge light on my Mouse.

Paul eyes me gloomily. "Just out of curiosity, how much did you make yesterday?"

"Two hundred apiece."

He's silent for a moment. "Maybe I should pick up a used lute and go into business for myself."

It's almost two-thirty when I swing off the upstairs escalator at Chatelet / Les Halles. The plaza has a lazy siesta feel: young couples sipping drinks at shaded café tables, a juggler in black tights twirling batons next to the fountain. Two people singing blues: a scrawny older white guy in a red-white-and-blue stovepipe hat and a black woman wearing a blue bandanna headwrap. He's strumming a Martin flattop, punctuating her words with tweets of rack-mounted harp; she's sitting just below him on the steps, rocking her shoulders, throwing herself into every belted note. His eyes twinkle as hers close. They're keeping up a conversation between verses. "Hey brown girl," he murmurs and she glances over her shoulder and goes "Uh huh" like she's heard this one before. "Where oh where did you sleep last night," he croons, and she shakes her head, pushes her horn-rimmed glasses up on her nose and says "Hey white boy"; he arches his eyebrows and twangs "What's that?" and she closes her eyes, sways, and answers him with a line about how lord knows she loves it when her sugar daddy holds her tight.

I don't notice the kids until the song ends; he hands her his hat while everybody claps and she explains that her name is Roselyn, his is David, and they're from New Orleans—"Twenty years ago we were *illegal* in New Orleans," she says, "but that's over now because we put our lives on the line just as people today are in South Africa"—and then she motions to them and they jump up. "This is David Junior," she says, putting her arm around the sleepy little boy, "but we all call him Stormy. And this is Autumn." Autumn is ten and willowy in her granny dress, with wavy brown hair and skin the color of coffee ice cream. Mom smiles, holds up the stovepipe hat. "If you've been enjoying our music please feel free to contribute *un peu d'argent.*" Then she hands it to Autumn and swings into another duet with Dad while the kids work their way around the circle, disappearing into a sea of coin-clutching tentacles. Mom pauses when the hat returns, empties it into a skirt-pocket, sets it on Dad's head, and picks up a mandolin while he sings about his St. Louis woman and her expensive tastes.

Somebody tugs at my hat. I spin to see Finney, cigarette dangling from his lower lip, battered acoustic guitar strapped to his back like a papoose.

"Surprise," he says.

"Ready to go?"

"Whenever you are."

We swing onto the escalator, gliding downward past a line of pretty girls: prim-mouthed French girls, ebony Senegalese beauties with plaited hair in whorled buns, girls from North Africa with darting brown eyes and skin like turbinado sugar. Do all of them have boyfriends? We curve through several tunnels, glide down a second escalator, bounce onto a Metro platform faintly perfumed with the rancid-dogshit smell of oxidized rubber wheels. Empty tracks stretch off into shadows; we throw ourselves into plastic bucket seats and tune up while Finney lays out the game plan. The basic principles of Metro-busking are easy. The train pulls in, you hop on, the doors close, the train pulls out. The next sixty seconds are yours. You smile and say "Bonjour messieurs et dames"—the frog bastards love it—and kick into your best song. The trains whine a bit; you've got to shout or you won't be heard. Jump around, put on a show. After half a minute swing into Phase Two: bottling. Take off your hat, make a quick circuit, wave it under their noses. Some will give, some won't. No way of predicting. The main thing is, you've got to finish up your bottling run just as the train is pulling into the next station. If you wait too long to bottle, they'll flee and you won't make a fucking cent.

The train-incoming buzzers sound. Finney jumps up and hits a chord. Suddenly anxious, I pull my hat low and look for something else to bottle with. An empty O'Kitsch Coke cup in a trash bin draws my eye; I snag it, two harps bulging in each hip pocket. The train glides to a stop, sliding steel drawers whoosh open, Finney and I swing in. A dozen people scattered through the car: tittering school-girls in navy cardigans, three olive-skinned men with sparkling eyes, a pale young woman garbed in fashionable downtown black, white-shawled grandmothers with plump frumpy legs swathed in support hose. We're strangers in a strange land. Let's hit it.

The train jerks forward just as Finney hits it, staggering me. My hat tumbles into a grandmother's lap. I rescue it, apologizing awkwardly, yanking it back onto my head as Finney keeps time. Then I sing.

The first few seconds are down-in-flames time, but when I come back in, my voice is clear and strong. I'm standing on the ped-als of a racing bike and feeling the sweet flow as the cranks drive down and around. One of the North Africans winks. My first steps away from Finney are tentative—swivel like Elvis or aim at the sky like Dizzy?—and then the music swallows me and I'm yelping at the girls until they giggle, closing my eyes and goose-honking when one of the old ladies glares. Don't let my act fool you, I think, opening my eyes. I'm a nice young man. Would this voice lie? *There* you go.

Finney nods—time to bottle—and I work back down the aisle, Coke cup swiveling, harp and hand masking the bottom half of my face. Nothing from the schoolgirls, but Miss Downtown surprises me with two francs, and the North African make a point of digging down for choice coins. I give them a cowboy nod as my cup clinks.

The train slows. The grandmothers adjust their shawls; every-body else rises and drifts toward the doors. I slide to a stop next to Finney, sweating, trying not to grin too broadly.

"The bitch is back," he says, eyeing our take.

"Thanks."

"You've done this before?"

"Always wanted to."

The face he makes is more grimace than smile. "I remember when I felt like that."

After riding the rails all afternoon, our groove is hot and tight. We've split up after a post-busking Coke—Finney has to switch out his axe for his electric back at Jorg's, I have to hit up the pensione for my Mouse. Other acts have been jockeying all afternoon; the cafes around Les Halles are humming with strolling guitarists and flute-players doing their best to charm spare change out of the front rows. Accordionists in ruffled shirts, whirling gypsy violinists. A guy in a tuxedo and dark sunglasses sawing a violin bow across a floppy strip of sheet metal to make haunting dreamy moans. The Fete de la Musique is in full swing; we need our heavy artillery.

When I get back to the Beaubourg, Finney is huddled on his amp at the top of the plaza, smoking. I set down my Mouse and daypack.

"Finney my man."

He barely glances up. "Right on time."

I make a quick busker's scan. A half-dozen Andean Indians down in front where we killed the day before—strumming uku-leles, tooting panpipes, beating tom-toms. A guy in a top hat tin-kling a piano-on-wheels. Caricaturists sprawled across the flats. The Beaubourg is lit up like a transparent computer-bank undergoing major renovation—anodized aluminum struts criss-crossing the front, a grid of green and yellow lights glinting through hundreds of latticed windows. Every inch of plaza seems to have been claimed.

"Damn."

"We're fucked up the ass."

I notice an empty spot on the upper corner, where the walkway goes through.

"Come on," I say, scooping up my Mouse.

"What's that?"

"Up by JiffiCrepes."

He slowly rouses himself. "Fucking Peruvians. Like a fucking plague."

I swing away and jostle through the crowd until I reach our spot. The Peruvians are down in the valley now. Finney trudges into view; I throw down my stuff and scoot off to buy a bottle.

I dart down the block, past Whaam! t-shirts, FastBurger, and a Quick plastered with posters for the QuickPoulet Minwich. There's a farmer's market across the street; I dodge in front of a guy on a moped wielding a baguette like a jouster's lance and cut through the door.

The place smells like freshly-turned earth. Bunches of new carrots with feathery green tops, tight-lipped old women in grey smocks picking through mounds of fuzzy peaches. I veer towards the wine-rack. Five francs, seven, ten. The seven-franc bottle has elegant little clumps of purple grapes, burnished gold lettering. Merifleau Côtes du Rhône. I grab it and head for the checkout line.

There's a young couple ahead of me. Arm around her waist, he's squeezing her ass. She's leggy and tan with full flared lips. They share a laugh. She's purring as she curls into him. Why can't happy couples leave me *alone*, goddammit? I slap down a handful of change and spin into the street with my bottle.

Finney is tuning up when I get back. I unzip my daypack and fish around for the Swiss Army knife, suddenly proud. He may have played with everybody in Paris but he's my guitar man tonight.

"You wanna hit?" as I crouch and pull out my knife.

"My stomach's a bit queasy, actually."

I center the corkscrew and twist, squeeze the bottle between my thighs and yank. *Snock.* Take a long gulping swallow, the wine sliding down smooth and warm like the fermented juices of some slaughtered wild beast. Belching quietly, I set the bottle next to my Mouse, unzip my daypack and pull stuff out like a lover stripping by the side of the bed. Get naked and slide in. I untangle cables and hook up the digital delay. Squeeze the footpedal. Testing one two. The fullness and presence. We're gonna fucking *slaughter* this whole goddamn—

I shiver and look up: girls in Guess jeans and curvy white t-shirts floating by. Red wine burning down through me. Another gulping slug and I clank the bottle onto the cobblestones, scrabble through jumbled harps, then leap up and stagger, hovering, clasping my A-harp and mike. I bite down on a low note. The animal groans. I lower my hands. "We in business or what?"

"We might want to tune up."

He twangs his E as I sound mine. A couple of guys in rainbow t-shirts plop down on the cobblestones, trading a bottle. Finney strums. It always comes down to now: this shiver of an instant before you throw yourself to the wind.

I slam into the turnaround and our sound erupts, fanning across the cobblestones. Within seconds we're the twin poles of an electromagnet, receding skeins of faces bending and curling around us like iron filings. "Welllllll," I sing, as my amped echoey voice breaks across the crowd:

> Welllllll...
> One and one are two...two and two are four...
> The way I love you girl you will...never know...
> Come on...baby don't you want to go...

Back to the saaaaame old place...sweet home Chicago.

Smiles of delight swirling around me as I stalk the circle heaving taut springy phrases up from down low. *Stare at them while you're singing.* I pace like a caged animal as the evening pours through me, a mysterious wine-drenched city throbbing into sundown, other acts buzzing faintly on all sides.

We crest to a finish and cut it off. The applause is a drug as I gulp more wine, snatch up my D-flat harp, and swing into "Take You Downtown." Every lick is two steps higher, clearer, more deliciously edged with harmonics from overdriven preamp circuits and a speaker-coil blown wide as fresh currents surge through:

> I'm gonna take you downtown and put clothes on your back....
>
> I'm gonna take you downtown and put clothes on your back....
>
> I love you girl...gonna buy you anything you like....

That sweet knotted ache when you're falling in love and she moans softly as your lips meet, her eyes are shining and you're grinning, you want to scoop her up and run into the street, spin cartwheels, leap up on fire hydrants, swing her through the door of a boutique so you can watch while she works the dress rack, holds a bright red sundress up to the swell of her chest, eyes herself in the mirror, swivels, brushes her hair back, tells you to hold on, ducks into the changing-room, and steps out looking so sweet and innocent and voluptuous and alive with her bare shoulders and arms—such a strong delicious female animal— that you want to strip off the dress and bury your face in her belly and breasts—

Then it all falls apart! Don't you see? I swing back around the circle, hungry faces swaying after me. Finney's keeping time and I'm reaching down, shouting

> Bye bye girl if I don't see you no more....
> Bye bye girl if I don't see you no more....
> Well I love you girl and I can't stand to see you go....

You're skiing down a slope where every blue-note is a mogul and you're working your edges hard, shooting for the sweet spot between major and minor where the world suddenly flies open and the truest thing you know rises to meet you—the sweetness in your aching throat, the musky smell of her breath on your pillow the night she moves out.

We sail out of "Take You Downtown" into more bursting applause, a smear of eyes crouching on the cobblestones behind me as I spin to grab my bottle and drink deeply, scooping up a D harp and kicking into "Key to the Highway":

> I got the key...to the highway....
> Billed out...I'm bound to go....
> I'm gonna leave here running because...walkin's most too slow....

A girl is holding out an orange frisbee like a church collection plate. She scatters coins in it and gingerly steps forward, smiles awkwardly and begins working her way around the circle. Finney scans the crowd, face sickly as a frog-belly. I settle my hat, chest swelling:

> Just give me one...one more kiss darlin'....
> Just before I go....
> 'Cause when I leave this time, lord I...won't be back no more....

The girl slips past me, crouches at Finney's case and empties the frisbee in a silvery cascade. I rock back, stamp the cobblestones, draining the last drop:

> I said so long...see you tomorrow....
> I must be on my way....
> I'm gonna roam this old highway...until my dying day....

I duckwalk towards Finney, blowing long yelping clusters, the two of us floating in a pool of orangey cobblestoned light. A shower of blue notes edged with thick glassy harmonics, the pressure of his beat driving me on:

> I got the key...to the highway....
> Billed out...I'm bound to go....
> I'm gonna leave here runnin' because....

and on *because* I give him the signal and he cuts off his chord as my voice sails on—

> ...walkin's most too slow....

before we come crashing back in, two starving cats pouncing on the same fleeing mouse.

Our final note is still ringing when I notice Jorg, hips at a jaunty angle, muttonchops bristling as he stands on the edge of our circle, arms folded. Finney slips out from under his guitar strap and veers towards him.

"Alriiiiight," I gasp as applause washes over us. "Thank you. Merci beaucoup. Je m'appelle McKay et je viens de New York—"

Whooooo!

"—je viens de New York. Et mon ami Finney vient de Londres."
I hold out my hand.

Finney glances up at his name, murmurs something to Jorg. Jorg quickly slides away. I'm spinning, crouching, raking through the jumble of harps, snapping up my E-flat. *I'm gonna pack my suitcase, move on down the....*

Finney is hovering. "Look, I've got an errand to run."

"*Now?*"

"No way round it, really."

"What the hell are you talking about? We're gonna lose all our momentum!"

"We'll work up a crowd when I get back."

His sunken white cheeks. I'm speechless.

"You don't need me," he says as a hundred pairs of eyes cradle us hungrily. "Just keep right on and you'll make a killing."

"It's not the same, man."

"Don't be so fucking uptight." He was already spinning away. "Keep an eye on my Strat. We can divvy up later."

I flap my hands helplessly.

"Brilliant." He squeezes through parted shoulders and disappears into the roar of the festival.

Forty-five minutes later I'm sitting on my Mouse, popping my thumb in and out of the empty wine bottle. Finney's guitar case is propped open where he left it. Our crowd is long gone. It's a warm, delicious evening. Other acts are doing good business. The Peruvians are thumping. Panpipes whistling, ukuleles plunking. A chorus of native voices chanting in unison. Roars every time they finish a song. The festival is slowly winding down.

A soft rustle makes me look up. Jorg is squatting next to me, hands between his thighs.

"Ca va?"

I stare at the rat-like incisors jammed under his mustache. "J'attends Finney."

He splays fingers on the cobblestones. "Il y a une petite probleme."

A little problem? What, death by asphyxiation after kinky sex play?

"Il reste chez moi." He smiles sheepishly, clasps his hands like a pillow and tilts his head. "Il dorme."

"Il *dorme?*"

He mimes the gesture of injecting himself. "Il se shoot, il s'endorme." He shrugs, spreads his hands. "He can not play musics when he sleeps."

For a moment I think about smashing him across the face. Then all I want to do is get away. I set the bottle down, stand up and stretch. I nod at Finney's guitar. "Tu va prendre ses choses?"

"Bien sur."

I stare at the layered coins lining the battered cardboard case. Suddenly I'm falling to my knees, raking them into a pile, grabbing my daypack, heaving it into my lap, unzipping the outer pocket, scooping up my share in a heavy double handful. A few coins clink onto the cobblestones; I toss them in, zip up, shoulder the bag as I grab my Mouse.

Jorg smiles in confusion. "You go so fast?"

"Take it easy, dude," I bark, grabbing the empty bottle and spinning away. I wrist-snap it into a trashcan. It explodes in a shower of broken glass. I can hear the Peruvians thumping after I've rounded the corner and half-walked, half-run down the block.

—told me this unbelievable story last night before you showed up at Le Mazet, Paul says. We're standing at the top of the Beaubourg plaza. It's the day after the Festival, our last day in Paris; a cool Sunday breeze has sprung up.

What's that?

Well *apparently*— He stresses the word, gestures at a six-foot high beige pillbox. *Apparently* some unsuspecting schlep came up, deposited his franc-and-a-half, waited for the hydraulic door to swing open, and was confronted with a dead baby.

No joke. A lost child wandered in shortly after they were first installed, closed the door, made peepee, pressed the flush-lever, then tried to open the door and couldn't. At which point the flush-mechanism kicked into gear. The mechanism on these state-of-the-art French potties happens to work by flipping the floor-sink-and-toilet assembly up and around into a sterilizing chemical bath, followed by a rinse and infrared drying cycle. So when Unsuspecting Schlep came along and deposited his franc-and-a—

You're joking.

Blue in the face and very dead.

Jesus. Hey, you wanna hit the top before we go?

We're strolling down across the plaza and through sliding glass doors, swinging around onto the escalator. Greenhouse smell of trapped air as we glide up into the clear Plexiglas tube. The plaza falls away, shrinking into a nubbly brown rectangle bordered with green fluff. A scattering of tourists, like brightly-colored bits of lint.

We step off the top, lean against the safety railing. The city is spread out below: squared gingerbread towers of Notre Dame, a junk-yard of jumbled rooftops, the Seine winding off into the distance.

There's the Eiffel Tower, I say.

We stare for a moment. It looks like the sort of thing you might play jacks with if you had a pink rubber ball.

I certainly got my exercise today, man.

Come to Paris and collapse your arches.

I wave him away. You'll eat a nice dinner, you'll get a good night's sleep, everything will be fine in the morning.

Speaking of the morning.

I was leaning towards a small Ferrari, although I'd be willing to settle for anything with four—

Holding up his hand. This is what we have to talk about.

Yo.

Remember my friend Kenna up in Geneva?

The mink from McGill. The cutie.

He grimaces, draws himself upright. Turns out she's flying to Greece at the end of this week for a month.

Huh. So you think we oughta head up there instead of the Riviera.

He takes a deep breath.

He's training it up there tomorrow morning; I'm heading south to St. Tropez or wherever. Skinny bikinis, women who sleep with the wolves. A week on my own to play the blues and debauch. We'll reconnect Monday in Bologna, take a train to Florence, do every last slimy disgusting thing down there we were planning on doing.

He's shrugging, avoiding my eyes. Not to mention that neither of us speaks a word of Italian.

Got it, I hear myself murmur. It makes sense to do that part of the trip together, I'm just—

Taking a deep breath, losing myself in a patchwork field of tarpaper and tinplate.

—would have said something last night but you were obviously in no shape.

I say nothing. The escalator thrums behind us. I'm staring at the plaza. Patch of cobblestones where Finney and I played last night is on the left. Back wall of JiffiCrepes, trash can where I threw the wine bottle. Busker's holiday.

Bologna, I murmur.

Bologna in seven days.

You better get laid, man. You better get fucking keelhauled by that goddamn—

Son, he drawls.

Rock me baby?

Like my back ain't got *no* bone.

S even twenty-three on Monday night and I'm whirling around my hotel room. TGV means Tres Grande Vitesse: fastest train in the West. A quick piss into the bidet—no time for the toilette down the hall–and I'm back onto the streets of Avignon, Panama yanked low, harps bulging in my hip pockets. New town, new life.

Two tanned young guys in white tennis shorts are bouncing in my direction: a short muscle-bound stud with a Roman nose, bulging out of his Gold's Gym singlet; a tall slim Romeo with moussed black hair and mustache, pink Lacoste collar flipped up. He sees my hat, cocks a finger.

Harmonica! he says. Da Pompidou Center.

You're from Paris? I say, incredulous.

I just came down last night. Where's your buddy with da gee-tar?

Things, ah…. They didn't work out.

Muscles jerks his chin. Where you from, man?

New York City.

Aaaaaaaaay, whaddya know.

I'm smiling. You sound like you're from that neck of the woods yourself.

That neck of the woods! he honks. I'm from Long Island.

Lawn*guy*lint, I echo.

He breaks into another clean white grin. So you're my home-boy? The name's Joey.

McKay, I say as he crushes my hand.

His friend with the mustache nods. Michel. From Montreal.

He says it like a native. I glance at Joey. Parlez-vous francais?

Whaddya think, Michel? Should we tell this guy about the top-less swimming pool?

I don't know about dis, Michel says, stroking his mustache.

We're standing on the sidewalk next to a café terrace. You guys hungry? I ask.

Joey pats his stomach. We just pigged out.

Thirsty? Hey, wine's on me.

They glance at each other. Joey flaps his hand. I don't know, man. I'm like semi-trashed already. I might get rowdy.

Dinner is over and we're strolling up through the middle of a café-rimmed plaza, bumping shoulders and goofing, cherchaying les dames.

Yo guys, check it out, Joey mutters. Three nymphets wander aimlessly past us: pastel sundresses, tan shoulders. Arms folded across young breasts. One bursts into giggles, covers her mouth.

Howyadoin', girls? Joey is crinkling his baby blues, flashing his Sly Stallone grin.

Americans! they cry. The word echoes through the warm June night.

Bailey, Marybeth, and Adele from the Louise Magee School for Girls in New Orleans and they are *so* bored, forty-seven of them plus three boys and six chaperones and they've been traveling through all these different cities in France in this big ol' bus with nobody to talk to, except Adele always talks to the French because she's Cajun and— where are *y'all* from? Joey leans towards me: We're probably gonna get in deep shit for dealing with jailbait but hey, what the fuck. Soon everybody is talking about how the Pont d'Avignon is really only half a bridge sticking into midriver. Marybeth points when I ask: Just walk down through the town wall and you cain't miss it.

Bailey's waving frantically and suddenly the whole giggling, sweet-smelling flock is swooping down. Pleated white shorts, lemon-yellow espadrilles, sunglasses pushed back on heads, Magnolia-blossom accents rustling and cooing. I've got seven or eight around me, preening. Joey and Michel each has a flock. Now *where* did y'all say you were from? a hoarse brunette keeps asking, fumbling with her cigarettes. Did y'all say y'all were from New *Yuuwwwrrrk*? She makes it sound like a creamy brown-sugar praline that softens and throbs on your tongue before dissolving. Joey is styling and profiling like a lifeguard at Jones Beach; Michel's teeth are flashing under his black mustache. Euro-preps with gold chains and penny loafers eye us enviously as they stroll by.

Girls! a voice calls out and we look up to see the chaperones, four or five in shirtwaist dresses and tennis sneakers working on ice cream cones. The girls groan. Time to go. But it's only ten! we cry. They shrug: Ten-thirty curfew. Then they're gone—touching our bare arms, blowing kisses and shouting goodbyes as they float back across the plaza like an outgoing tide.

We stare at the space where they just were. Silverware clinking on plates. The murmur of cafés.

Yeah well, says Joey. Whaddya want from high school? We weren't gonna get laid anyway.

We punch shoulders and slap faces, bounce towards the nearest table, throw ourselves into chairs and holler for more Côtes du Rhône red. The waiter swings into view with three tumblers on a tray. We salute and toss back. A breeze rustles the chestnut tree overhead.

A second round is ordered, then a third. The stuff is smooth, flinty. We're wading deep into guy talk. The topless swimming pool, looking for pussy, dealing with girlfriends. They both have ladies back home. Not that it makes any difference while I'm here, Joey chuckles, arms stretched overhead. I fill them in: Helen's affairs, out on my own after five years. I lean towards Joey: Forty-seven girls from New Orleans and I didn't get one fucking phone number! He smiles vaguely, eyes on the table. Glances at Michel.

After five or six glasses I stand up, tottering, and shoulder my daypack. They're heading down to Barcelona in the AM; they tell me what beach to look them up on if I get the urge to check out Español babes. Joey is rubbing his peeling tan shoulders, we're slapping fives. Take care, man. I'm chuckling as I spin away towards the bottom of the plaza, spotlights smearing across my eyes. Digging into my hip pocket, curling fingers around my harp and squeezing. Stubbing my toe and staggering. Catching myself just before I fall.

Tuesday noon and town is behind me; I'm heading towards the pool. Blowing harp across Pont Daladier with the highway disappearing into countryside up ahead, water swirling green and froth-tipped down below. Swinging through a gap in the guardrail, trotting down endless metal stairs. Sour tang of damp steel as I sink into shady coolness. Blue notes swelling, echoing against the girders; I'm hitting bottom and crunching onto gravel, Mouse swinging from my hand.

Hey, a voice calls.

Two bodies under the bridge scrambling to their feet behind a chain-link fence.

Have you got some fire? Guy on the left raises a pack of Marlboros as he bounces toward me. Unlit cigarette dangling from his lips, guitar propped on his shoulder like a club. Front tooth chipped into a sharp triangle.

Sorry, I don't smoke.

I'm dying, man, he chuckles, clasping his chest. You've braw-wwk me poor hearrrt. Jerks his chin at his friend's dangling bottle. You wanna come round back and have a drink? His friend is a pixie in a dusty black sweater, blond dreads littered with straw.

Nah, thanks.

Lord Jesus! he cries, staring at my Mouse.

Battery-powered, I say, tooting my harp.

I sketch out my self-appointed mission in bad French and the pixie grows excited. He knows Finney. He knows Jorg. He knows that whole crew up in Paris, or seems to. Le Mazet, Danny Fitzgerald, the Lost Wandering Blues and Jazz Band! He waves his hands and chatters like a chickadee on speed. As far as I can tell, there's a week-long festival in Avignon starting tonight and people are pouring into town from all directions. Everybody throwing money if you play music! My friend play not so good the guitar, he says in French, shrugging.

What are you saying about me, you lying Algerian bastard? chipped-tooth rasps, pulling away from the fence as he coughs and doubles over.

Nah, just telling me you play guitar.

I've only been at it a week, he says. He props it on his lifted knee, frets a random handful of strings. His strumming hand has one finger—a skinny claw-like thumb with nail—and four shapeless

Thalidomide bumps. He makes tuneless noise for a moment, then grins. I've been doing twice as well up in town since I picked it up.

The pixie raises his finger. Ecoute! Tu dois trouver l'Africain dans sa chaise roulante! La guitare—il joue formidable! Les blues, n'importe quoi! Il chant aussi! Oh oh oh! Tu dois jouer ensemble!

What's that, Babouche? his friend mutters.

Some African guy in a wheelchair? I say.

Him? He's worse off than me.

Babouche seems to think we should team up.

If you can find him, sure. He's always whoring around.

I glance at Babouche. Tu peux lui trouver?

He swells up like a puffball. Babouche va le faire.

Alriiiiight, I say, hooking his fingers through the fence. I let go and nod at chipped-tooth. And you're...English?

I'm Welsh, he says proudly, making the word into a question by giving it a little lift at the end. Sticks a couple fingers from his good hand through. The name's Duncan.

Babouche! chimes Babouche as he clutches our clasped hands.

Late afternoon and I'm blowing my way uphill from the river, Mouse banging against my hip, face sheened with coconut oil and sweat.

I'm gonna take you downtown...put clothes on your back.... I'm gonna take you down—

The plaza opens up to embrace me. Band of Peruvians thumping straight ahead, winds whistling through the Andes. Crowds eddying, swirling.

PHEEEEER-WHEEEET! like somebody hailing a cab.

Veering across the plaza, bumping elbows with Babouche as I plunk down my Mouse on the paving stones. The African's hair is a tangle of brownish-black dreads; legs wasted and useless, crossed at the knee-knobs. Electric guitar straddling his lap, head lowered, he's twanging, adjusting. Small black amp next to his wheelchair, guitar-case open at his feet.

Excuse-moi, I murmur. On m'a dit que tu joue les blues.

He glances up, takes me in, chuckles. Ahhhhhhhh, he lion purrs, you're younger than I thought. He nods at Babouche. Your little friend here keeps buzzing around my head, you know—telling me that I must not leave until the American with the white hat is arrived. He waves at my harmonica. You play?

I'm grinning. You ready to make some money?

...because I'm HEEEEE-EEEERE....EVERYBODY knows I'm here...well I'm the hoochie-coochie maa-aaaaan....EVERYBODY knows I'm—

We're shoulder to shoulder, plugged in, ready to rock. I'm wrenching a fat, greasy, stop-time riff out of the funky spit-soaked bowels of my harp.

Ba-bump-a-ba-BUMP...
Gypsy woman told mah mothaaa...
Before ah was born
You got a boychild comin'...
He's gonna be a son-of-a—

Voice like a Malian prince crossed with Lightnin' Hopkins, butterfly-jungles of Madagascar crossed with the darkest, richest bottom land in the Mississippi Delta—skittering down the levee on an August dog-day, sweat dripping off your breastbone and the thick heady catfish smell of freshly-dredged river-muck slapping you across the face.

Ba-bumpa-ba-BUMP…
I got a black cat bone
I got a mojo too
I got a John the Cockeroo
I'm gonna mess with—

Tumbling over themselves to reach us, five rows deep. Babouche is hovering, eyes burning.

Well I'm the hooochie-coooochie maaaa-aaaaan….EVERYBODY knows I'm heeeere….

The African nods at me. I'm adjusting the fit between harp and mike, taking a deep breath. The grain of his voice slicing across the heat in my pool-drenched heart, wrenching a couple of jammed-together notes down into the blue-zone:

Ba-bumpa-ba BUMP:
On the seventh day
Of the seventh month
The seventh doctor say…

Babouche gesturing frantically. I'm clasping harp to mike with one hand, lifting off my Panama with the other.

…He was born for good luck
And that you'll see
I got seven hundred dollars
NOW DON'T YOU MESS WITH—

Voila, he chirps, handing it back. The straw crown is distended, heavy with coins. We're hurling the song into an ending, cheers bathing us like tide. The African leans towards me and chuckles as he wipes sweat off his face.

That was *pretty*, man. Do you know—ahhh, let me think. He shifts in his wheelchair as the crowd simmers, lifts one withered leg and settles it. Strokes his chin. Do you know "Help Me" by Sonny Boay Weelyahmsun?

What key?

B-baymol. B flat for you.

You got to help me, babe.....I can't do it all by myself...you got to heeeeelp me, babe....I can't do it all by my—

We've been drinking our profits all evening, working our charms on girls at neighboring tables. We've hooked a pair of townies. Now we're stumbling back to their place. Solomon leads the way—racing ahead, spinning to face us he rears back in his chair with dreads swinging crazily.

Natalie's carrying his guitar case, as long as she is tall. Her eyes crinkle and burn when she grins.

And you will stay how much the time in Avignon? the bucktoothed girl murmurs as we stroll, blonde poodle-curls swinging away from her face.

I flap my hand. Two days, three days.

Long legs in tight jeans. Guess on the butt pocket. Breasts floating freely under her half-unbuttoned shirt.

Wellllll...two and two are four...four and two are six...come on baby don't you...be too quick.

I'm lying on a sleeping bag on a hard wooden floor in a darkened room, sheet pulled up to my armpits. Cecile's next to me, breasts veiled, head turned toward me on the pillow, eyes wide.

I reach out, brush her hand.

A soft moan as she slides against me. Fingers caressing my jaw, lips hungry for mine. I'm hooking my fingers under her panties, cupping a sweet heavy handful of bare ass as we roll. I'm hard, she's wet, neither of us is saying a word as she spreads her legs and guides me, gasping as I slide partway in and pause—supporting my weight, gazing down.

The startled grateful look in her eyes.

Trying not to think about Helen, I close my eyes and push my lips against hers, tongue swirling against the back of her splayed front teeth. Her hips buck upward. A sickening numbness spreads through me.

Attends, I whisper as I lift my head, breaking the silence. Wait.

She's staring up at me. Panting, confused.

Easing myself out, lowering myself onto the sleeping bag and throwing an arm across her sweat-slick chest. She clamps her lips down over her protruding teeth, chin trembling.

Je ne peux pas le faire, I whisper. I can't do it.

She stares at me bitterly, then lifts my arm off and rolls away. Curls around herself and lies quietly. So quietly I can hear my heart beating in the moment before she starts to cry.

Early Wednesday evening. Warm velvety air on the Place de l'Horloge; an out-of-tune sax honking "The Maple Leaf Rag." Solomon is beaming as I come up—half-finished glass of beer in one hand, smoldering Gauloise in the other. Dreads tied back like wooly brown sticks. He's leaning back in his wheelchair at our café.

Ahhhhh. Ca va?

I make the mezzo-mezzo sign. Je suis fatigue´.

A young white guy with a chiseled face is slouching in the chair next to him, arms folded.

You're wiped out from making love with this girl last night, Solomon chuckles, slapping my hand playfully.

Nah, it wasn't like that.

He winks at the white guy. Voila l'harmoniciste de blues Americain.

The guy gives me a quick once-over—Panama hat, Mouse amp, cutoffs—and nods. Tres authentique.

Jean-Pierre plays harmonica with my band in Strasbourg, Solomon purrs, leaning forward to stub out his cigarette. He's very interested to hear you playing with me tonight.

I set my Mouse on the paving stones, hook my daypack off my shoulder as I fall into a chair. Tu va jouer avec nous?

He purses his lips, smiles faintly. Je suis spectateur.

He has come to steal me, Solomon chuckles. The band is always doing this. I'm having too much good times by myself, too many girls, they send him out to drag me home. He takes a mouthful of beer, holds it like a charge of mouthwash, then swallows.

I stick up my finger, catch the eye of a waiter swinging past. Un Fisher demi, s'il vous plait. He nods and keeps moving. I glance at Solomon. Alors, tu va revenir a Strasbourg?

Non, on doit jouer un concert en Barcelona demain après-midi. He gives me a tripped-out hippie grin. I have a giiiiiig, maaaaaan. We take a train very late tonight.

Jean-Pierre nods, avoiding my eyes. The saxophonist at the far end of the plaza honks his pedal-tone, done.

Well, Solomon says briskly. He glances right, catches sight of a white girl in a pink halter top wandering across the plaza, stares hungrily. Glances at me. You like this one?

I wouldn't kick her out of bed, I say, trying to smile.

Stumbling along the rutted dirt road away from the swimming pool after my daily fix. It's Thursday afternoon, blustery; my train to Cannes leaves in twenty-five minutes. The Rhone is grey and seething, scudding with white wavelets. Pack straps biting into my shoulders as the Mistral beats my damp hair into knots, singing to nobody but myself:

Good morning blues, blues how do you do. Five long years with one woman, and she had the nerve to leave me blue. Well I'm southbound...lord I'm coming home to—

Lifting my head at the clanging slap of guitar strings against the wind. Hesitating, then veering around a white stucco wall into the campgrounds. Picnic tables up ahead, campsites scattered through the woods veiled by scrubby brown trees.

I pause in the doorway of the laundry room. Sweet billowy smell of fabric softener, a line of dryers rolling and tumbling, couple of tan blondes in hiking shorts giggling into their hands as a bare-chested young guy with floppy straw hat hollers and grimaces in the middle of the room, thrashes at an old steel-string guitar:

> Oh...baby don't you want to go-ohhhhh...
> Oh...baby don't you want to go-ohhhhh...
> Back to the land of Californiaa...to my sweet home Chicago....

He's boom-drawling it, punking it up, sneering at his own voice as it shapes the words. Five or six voices rolled into one.

Duckwalking barefoot across the concrete floor. Grease-stained chinos, small bulbous nose. Face welted with acne-sores—he's glancing up at me, curling lips away from his teeth and nodding. I'm setting down my Mouse amplifier, squeezing fingers under my pack-belt as I reach into my hip pocket:

Welllll...

Six and two is eight...eight and two is ten...

If that bitch went and fucked him once she sure gonna do it again....

I'm cryin' hey...baby don't you want—

We're not in tune but nobody's complaining. Hamming it up like vaudeville hoofers—shoulder to shoulder, hatbrim to hatbrim. Pack's swinging crazily on my back; I'm blowing notes off the ceiling, off the walls.

Hey! Hey! Hey! Hey! he barks as he windmill-strums the last four chords. I'm screaming on my ten hole and BAM! the song's over. We're grabbing hands and chuckling, panting as the girls applaud. His palm is damp. Erect brown nipples on his skinny chest.

Well now that's alll-riiiiight, he drawls. I can uuuuuuuse you. His grin is exhilarating, demonic, sincere.

I've never heard anybody sing it like that, I say.

Sweet Home Chicago? Hell, I make up my own words when ah get bored.

I mean with the Robert Johnson part about back to the land of Californiaaaaa instead of back to the saaaame old plaaaaace....

Naaaah, he says cheerfully. Everything's the same anyway. We're all born to die.

This was nice music, one of the girls murmurs in an accented voice.

Yes, adds the other.

We look up. The one who said Yes has dizzyingly blue eyes and lips that need nibbling.

Ahhhhh, the guitarist drawls, scratching his belly. We're just gettin' warmed up. He catches sight of my Mouse. Heeeeyyyyy.

I smile as I heave my pack down off my shoulder. You know about these?

> Wellllll... he sings, hugging his guitar like a dance-partner as he dips away in a little barefoot two-step:
> Wellllll..
> We're goin' on a holiday now...we're gonna take a villa or a small chalet...
> Costa del...Magnifico...yeah the cost of livin's so damn low...

His straw hat flops off as he swings in a dizzy circle. He reaches down and scoops it up, slaps it back on, twists his way over to a pile of unfolded laundry sitting on a table, reaches in, heaves out a Mouse dripping with black socks, sets it on top of the pile, slaps off the socks, yanks out the charge-cord—which snakes up to a wall socket next to the washing machines—and swings it down off the table in one crazed twisting arc that deposits it neatly on the floor next to mine. Plastered across the back is a maroon bumper sticker which reads DON'T POSTPONE JOY. The black mesh front is scratched and dented; there's a birdshit-colored splotch on the speaker cone.

The girls giggle. He's grinning triumphantly, all teeth.

What's your name? I say.

You ready to do some damage up in town? he says.

Her name was Constanza—she had a torn-up apartment, great body for a forty-year old except for the scratches on her face, and a six-year-old kid named Laura. He tells me the story while we're having wine and stew at his campsite that evening. He never did sleep with the daughter. The mother wanted him to. The daughter was a child-model in Milan; that's where he'd met them, when he was killing time one afternoon before his all-night train to St. Tropez.

The way it all starts is, he's hanging out in a park near the Milano Centrale station minding his own business. Sitting on a bench, picking guitar, watching ducks in the pond nibble their own tailfeathers. He's dressed the same as he is now: straw hat from Beale Street, army surplus chinos, black wingtips from Goodwill, t-shirt that reads IF IT'S GOT TITS OR WHEELS, SOONER OR LATER YOU'VE GOT PROBLEMS. Mirrored sunglasses with one lens that's sorta cracked. Pretty suave for a twenty-one year old just-graduate of Memphis State.

Next thing he knows this lady is strolling around the edge of the duck-pond. She's wearing baggy green shorts and a silk shirt, fancy shoes. Killer legs. Just in front of her is this cute little girl with long black hair who keeps zipping in circles like a wind-up toy, kicking a plastic beachball onto the grass and chasing after it. The girl catches sight of him, slows down. He's humming the Dire Straits song about money for nothing and chicks for free. The lady comes up and sits down on the other end of his bench. Crosses her legs, brushes her hair out of her face. A few scratches—like she got caught on brambles—but she's not bad-looking. A little dried-up. Very tan. The tops of her boobs are sprinkled with freckles. That's the best thing about mirrored shades. He nods at her, smiles, keeps picking.

She sits there without saying a word while he hums a couple more songs. Oh Carol, Brown Sugar. He's not really doing it for her benefit, he kinda is. Meanwhile he's keeping an eye on the little girl as she chases her beachball around the bench. Swats it away with the neck of his guitar when it gets too close. He's still sorta tripping from the tab he popped on the train down from Zurich; the whole thing feels like some weird kind of croquet.

Anyway, he finally takes a break and pulls out his cigarettes. Offers one to the lady because he's a gentleman, heh-heh. She smiles and takes it. He can feel the class dripping off her fingertips; the blond streaks in her hair must have cost big bucks at some salon.

She asks him where he's from as he gives her a light—her accent is so strong he can barely understand the question—and he says Welllll, he's sorta from Illinois by way of Memphis although Paris and Amsterdam were pretty cool and he's been hearing a lot about the bullfights down in Spain. America, basically. Then he pulls off his shades and introduces himself: Billy Lee Grant, world famous bluesician and great-great-great grandnephew of Ulysses. Which just happens to be the twisted truth.

Well, the lady thinks this is great. She calls her daughter over. The kid's name is Laura; hell on wheels is putting it mildly. Simpering, pouting, acting like the whole world revolves around her navel. The mother can't get enough. Is beautiful, she keeps sighing. Bella, bella. My beautiful little baby. More beautiful than me when I am so young. The mother's name is Constanza Bugatti. She smiles when he asks; no relation to the sportscar. He sings a few bars of Baby You Can Drive My Car just for the hell of it. The spoiled little fuck throws her beachball in his face. He makes like he's gonna brain her, then grins. Cute little thing, ain't she? he says. My my my.

Turns out the cute little thing is just about to enter kindergarten and the mother is dying to get her into the American School in Milan. The admissions exam is at the beginning of August. The mother needs a tutor: somebody who will accompany her and her daughter to St. Moritz for six weeks, who will live, eat, and frolic with them at a modest but comfortable luxury resort—all at her expense—and who will, in exchange, instruct Laura for four hours every morning in the finer points of English conversation. She's looking off as she tells Bill this stuff. Gnawing on her fingernail. Does he have any idea where she might find such a person?

Welllll, he drawls. He once wrote a paper comparing "The Freewheelin' Bob Dylan" to *Naked Lunch*, which doesn't have much to do with teaching her little ravioli here how to speak American like a native but it just so *happens* that about three weeks ago he completed his degree in English at one of the finest liberal arts colleges in southwestern Tennessee. Plus he loves kids. Ol' Kidaroos.

Within fifteen minutes, she's inviting him back for dinner. He's already blown off his seven o'clock train, his Mouse and blanket-roll and spare pair of underwear are sitting on some shelf in the baggage checkroom at Milano Centrale. He figures he'll tag along and see what happens. Six weeks seems like a long time but you never know. At least he'll get a free meal out of it. Worse comes to worse he can always crawl back to the park and crash.

This is where the whole thing starts to get kinda surreal. It's weird enough walking through the streets of Milan at dinner-time with a couple of Italian females he barely knows and a guitar-case under his arm, especially when the females are smiling and hovering like he's some sorta wild animal they've just trapped. The mother keeps asking him what he wants to eat. Prosciutto? Melonay? They stop in front of a deli with big hams and cheeses hanging like bazookas in the window; he's supposed to watch Laura while Mom goes inside to buy supplies. The moment she splits the little twerp holds out her hand for his hat. He figures what the fuck, it's sorta his job now. He takes it off. She grabs it with both hands and yanks it down over her eyes like she's trying to rip her goddamn head right through it. He keeps his cool—holds out his hand, asks for it back. The girl gives him the most spoiled-rotten little devil-smile you've ever seen and goes No. At which point he mutters You little fuck and rips it away and she starts howling and the mother comes running out and he has to think up some story real quick and make stupid faces at the kid until she stops blubbering. There's no way in hell he's gonna spend six weeks with the little monster now. He's still up for dinner, though. He hasn't had a home-cooked meal in weeks.

They get back to Constanza's apartment building—she has to buzz them in through three different security doors, she says something about red terrorists and how the guy who owns Fiat lives on the floor below her—and then they're getting off the elevator and she's trotting down the hall with her ass swishing and Beatrice is playing pattycake with the beachball up ahead. She stops in front of a door, twists open the locks and lets him in. He can smell her perfume—like crushed dried roses—as he squeezes by. He walks into the living room and drops his guitar-case next to the puffed-up white sofa.

The place is sorta disorganized. Not dirty, just with books and files stacked on the floor, things that should be on shelves sitting on tables. Photo albums. She shows him one before dinner, when he's working on his third or fourth Chivas. It's full of pictures of her and the different princes and counts she used to party with in St. Moritz holding up champagne glasses and grinning. She's leaning over his shoulder and pointing them out as he turns the pages. Prince Rainier, Baron von Richtdorfer. Youngish guys in tuxedos with greased-back hair and long noses. A lot of skinny drunken blondes with satiny dresses falling off their tits. She shakes her head, kicks off her sandals. I knew Bardot, she says. Bianca, Caroline. All the bunch. She pouts and makes a fuck-it noise, waves her hand. I am shitted with the jet-setteurs, you understand? We go to St. Moritz this time but we don't see them. They're all shit. She points out one guy who used to be her husband. Viscount de Somebody. He looks just like the rest—same greasy-kid stuff hair, same shiny forehead. She shrugs; he's not a bad man. He sends money. Laura doesn't see him now for two years.

Dinner is pretty low-key: about five huge tomatoes sliced up on a plate with olive oil and salt, rolls with butter, the prosciutto she just bought, coupla cans of Heineken. Sort of an indoor picnic, to go along with the torn-up living room. The whole time he's eating she's talking a blue streak—complaining about her liver, worrying about how she's gonna afford this apartment now that she's on her own, bitching about how she had to sell the place at St. Moritz last winter to pay her bills and this is the first time she'll be staying in a hotel. She keeps touching the scratches on her cheeks and muttering about how she can't sleep at night. The sane life, she says: we will lead the sane life up at St. Moritz. Swimming, tennis. Long walks in the mountains. You, me, Laura: we will make like a family. You can have other girls if you want. I am too old for you, Laura is too young. What a pity!

It's starting to get a little creepy, but he's kinda sorry for her too. Take away the fancy clothes and streaks in her hair and she's one hurt puppy. He tries to cheer her up after dinner—they go into the living room, he pulls out his guitar and sings "Old MacDonald Had a Farm" the way Tom Waits would do it after the same number of drinks. She and Laura are laughing so hard they're almost crying. Then she makes him stop while Laura holds her hands overhead and does a little dance, spinning slowly in her purple bathing suit. Look at her legs! the mother whispers. Look at her body! More pretty than me when I am so young! She's staring at the kid like she's about to eat her alive. He's trying not to look but it's kinda hard not to, even if she is only six. Those perfect little thighs. Shit.

They fuck later, after she's put Laura to bed. He wasn't really planning on it, but she obviously has a nice body and it seems like it's supposed to happen. At least it isn't kinky shit involving the kid. They crawl between the sheets, he gets it up, she helps him stick it in. No big deal. Her mouth tastes dead. All that stuff about Italian women making great lovers is total bullshit; he's had fifty times better pussy from this skinny little black girl back home in Carbondale. Charlayne. Of course he was in love with her, which makes a difference.

In the morning everything gets weird. He's standing around the kitchen chewing on some toast she's made, drinking strong coffee. She's fussing with her daughter's hair and muttering in Italian. Nobody's said anything about St. Moritz but he's starting to feel like six weeks is pushing it. Two weeks he can see but there's no way he's gonna blow his whole summer in one spot, especially with the little kid giving him orders. Plus his Eurrail Pass would go to waste. He starts trying to explain this. She keeps combing Laura's hair, yanking at knots and muttering about how she just doesn't understand him, why can't he just speak English instead of talking like a peasant. He's gonna ruin her little girl. The more he tries to calm her down the worse it gets. Problems! she screams. Everything is for you a problem! The little twerp starts bawling. Suddenly this big old fuse in his chest goes pfffft. Lady, he mutters, *one* of us has a problem and it sure as hell ain't me. It takes him about ten seconds to grab his hat and guitar and get out. She's still in the kitchen as he slams the front door— shouting and waving her hands, yanking at her daughter's hair.

He gets back onto the street—it's a clear morning with lots of sun and fresh air, and for some bizarre reason he feels great. Stoked up, roaring, ready to leap on a train and shoot a thousand miles in any direction. He cuts in front of a trolley car and asks some newsstand guy where Milano Centrale is. The guy gives him this weird smile—he's small and brown with a mustache and flashing eyes, from India or Pakistan—and jerks his chin. You from America, my friend?

Yep, says Bill. Ah, the man says. My brother lives in New York City. Do you know this Times Square? Bill says Uh huh and the guy starts telling him how his brother owns some porno video shop on the corner of Broadway and 43rd Street, which happens to be just down the block from the spot Bill was busking for three days before he flew over to Paris, which is where my new life began, too. Small world. Anyway, that's what he was doing before he rolled down here and met me.

I'm goin' to New Orleans, won't be back no more...
Goin' back down south, child, don't you wanna go...
Woman I'm troubled, I be all worried in mind...
I just can't be satisfied and I just can't keep from cryin'...

We lie around our campsite after dinner—finishing up the second bottle of Côtes du Rhône red, working out killer endings for half a dozen songs, giving our Mouses a chance to suck fresh juice out of the laundry-room socket. We have the groove from hell, ninety-six hours before I'm supposed to meet back up with Paul in Bologna. The Riviera is in trouble. All able-bodied females between the ages of six-teen and sixty are fucked. Paper bags over the heads of the ugly ones. All we want to do is match musical souls—my harp-lines to his voice, like Little Walter and early Muddy—and rake in the profits. Ninety each this afternoon, plus the Swedish girls who gave us their addresses up in Gothenburg. Summer is here.

Around nine o'clock we suddenly get restless—we can almost taste the clean beautiful spaces up on the plaza, the prime busking spot in front of the Hotel de Ville—so Bill packs up his guitar, I clap harps into boxes and make a pallet for myself on one side of his tent with stacks of my folded t-shirts. He tosses me a sheet he's not using.

The inside of the tent smells like pine needles, mosquito repellent, drizzly grey mornings in the middle of forests. I crouch on hands and knees and breathe deeply, my throat suddenly tight. How long since I've spent a night in the woods? Then Bill gives a holler and I haunch back out, grab another handful of wild apricots from the branch dangling over the tent and take off after him.

We cruise out the front gate—my Mouse bouncing against my hip, Bill's hanging off his shoulder in the green canvas rucksack. He's wearing a fresh t-shirt: NO COMPUTER IS GOING TO REPLACE ME UNTIL IT LEARNS TO DRINK. We're passing the third bottle—the fourth's in my daypack—and getting extremely lewd when we suddenly notice the river. The Mistral has died down, the water has smoothed; it's this pure, velvety, glistening thing spread out at our feet. The Pont d'Avignon looms on the far side—four white stone arches hopscotching into midriver, roadway slicing across the top. The broken-off end is only fifty yards away. "Look at the lonesome river!" Bill booms in his Johnny Cash voice. "Look at the lonesome shaggy bridge!" He takes another swig and belches, hands me the bottle, drops his guitar case and rucksack and starts to strip. Straw hat, t-shirt, black wingtips. I ask him what he's doing; he grins as he peels off his chinos and bikini briefs. "Time to get nekkid, McKay," he drawls, dick dangling. He turns towards the river—a flash of bare ass in the twilight—and leaps in.

I stand there, heart smoking. He explodes through the surface and lets out a huge wahoo. "Ya big wimp!" he rags. "Kerouac would be playing water polo by now!" I never should have told him about my graduate work, but he's right. I knock off my hat, elbow out of my t-shirt and hesitate, then reach down and unzip my cutoffs, sliding them off in one quick motion along with my underpants and running shoes. It takes a terrific effort to stand up straight but I do.

The sky is lavender soft; the light breeze tickles my crotch hair. Bill's treading water and waiting for me. Penis to the world. I step barefoot onto the flattened weeds, then take a deep breath and hurl myself in.

The river swallows me like a cool green kiss. I'm almost sobbing when I burst through—gasping, wrenched, cradled, tingling. Bill is already splashing away, a flurry of strokes towards the diamond-shaped foot of the Pont. I'm halfway there, struggling against the drift, when he hits home. "Feel the slime on the lonesome stones!" he booms. I keep sidestroking. The distance keeps stretching out; cold currents envelop me as I push into midriver. The broken-off end suddenly looms, a ragged brick wall streaked with grime. No place to grab hold—Bill's working hard to stay even, holding position like a schooling fish as the water swirls past him. "Bumpy little ride there," he grins as I slide in next to him, gasping. I'm trying not to knee him in the balls as I tread water. He ducks below the surface, then explodes back through with a shake of his sopping head. "I'm just siiiiingin' in the raaaaaaiin!" he belts, jawbone dropped for extra bass.

"You're crazy!" I shout.

"Waaaaaughhahahaha!" he roars and suddenly he's diving underwater and grabbing for me and I'm panicking, kicking franti-cally as I lunge backward shouting No! and he's bobbing to the sur-face and guffawing, pretending it's all a joke while my heart heaves.

By the time we crawl back onto shore we're wiped out and reckless, burning like quarter-mile dragsters after a nitro run. "We're gonna destroy 'em!" Bill drawls as he staggers into his chinos. I rake my hands through my hair and giggle—no comb tonight, no shower, I want the smell of the river all over me, the wildness and coolness and flow. My balls are aching from the leap.

We hump up into town through darkened streets. The plaza is a whirl of spotlit cafes and strolling pedestrians fumbling with takeout crepes wrapped in white greasepaper. A Peruvian band is thumping and whistling to a big crowd in front of the Hotel de Ville. My heart sinks—seven Andean Indians, we'll be drowned out no matter where we set up—but Bill's all smiles; within five minutes he's made friends with Willie, the dark-haired little guy with punk-style shaved temples selling their cassette off to the side. "Ahhh," Willie nods when Bill holds up his guitar case. "You playa rockin roll." He eyes the bumper sticker plastered across the top—THIS CAR PROTECTED BY PIT-BULL WITH AIDS—and touches his heart. "We: Aymara. Speaking Eeenglish somatime. No Frenches." Bill hands him our wine bottle and starts in on a story about the afternoon he and his Filipino girl-friend were tripping at the Elvis Museum in Memphis and he sud-denly got this idea of running across the street to Graceland, signing his name and hers on the stone wall next to the sidewalk with a bottle of ketchup he'd stolen from the museum coffee shop and then climb-ing up and singing "Blue Suede Shoes" with air-guitar accompani-ment until security guards came out and grabbed him. He's standing with his arms folded as he tells Willie this, pushing his mirrored shades up on his nose. Willie drinks, nods his stone face.

We kick into gear the moment the Peruvians finish—I throw down my stuff, Bill jumps up on his Mouse and announces that Billy Lee Grant and his Bottom Stompers will be coming up next and parents with young kids oughta think about hustling them off to bed because this ain't a family show, folks, it's lowdown nasty, smelly, funky, dirty-rotten ol' junkyard-dawg *blues* and we sure don't wanna offend anybody. Heh heh.

That hooks everybody. Our only problem is the tribe of saf-fron-robed Hare Krishnas who cha-cha-cha up behind us. The head guy approaches Bill—fastidiously, like he's afraid of catching a virus—and tells him the Hare Krishnas always play this particular spot on Thursday nights. Bill grins like a Texas used-car salesman as he straps on his axe. "Hell," he drawls, "if you boys wanna jam we can always use the percussion." "But our music is more *spiritual,*" the guy whines, wringing his hands. Bill is just draining our third bottle. He swallows, flashes his teeth under his mirrored shades, walks over to a metal trashcan, whips out his Swiss Army knife, flicks out the file, scores the neck of the bottle with a focused twirl, snaps the knife shut, glances up at the crowd, raises the bottle over his head like a torch, snarls, and swings it downward and sideways on a perfectly-calibrated vector—pwrassssshh!—so the glass below the score-line explodes like a fragmentation bomb into the hollow metal can and he's left holding a three-inch bottleneck with a couple of jagged spurs. He crouches to grind these smooth against the paving stones, shoves the bottleneck onto his ring finger and stands up, chuckling. The Krishna leader blanches. A tap on my elbow: Babouche smiling hungrily. Same deal as yesterday? Duncan's giving me a grinning thumbs-up with his Thalidomide flipper. Bill leans in to ask if I'm ready; I stare at my bulging face in his cracked lens—Panama hat, swamp-hair—and mumble Yeah. Then he spins volume controls until his Mouse is creaking, grunts a quick four-count—Anh! Anh! Anh! Anh!—and plows into "Hellhound on my Trail."

He does his thing—grimacing, groaning, kneeling, yelling at his guitar like there's a coiled snake trying to burst out through his fingertips and the fretboard is the only thing holding it back; I'm reaching down and hauling up a choked stream of edgy, yanked notes that blossom in my throat like kisses veering into complaints mushrooming into sobbed curses. We're trading choruses of "Sweet Home Chicago." I close my eyes. Bill takes over:

> Wellll...ten and five is fifteen...
> six-and-a-half times two is thirteen...

I don't like youuuuu and you don't like meeeee....

Babouche taps my elbow; I yank off my hat and hand it to him. A carp-and-algae whiff. Our groove is faltering, I'm glancing at Bill, he's pulling off his straw hat and howdydoing as he hands it to a large bare-chested guy with dark hairy legs who I could swear I know, and do. It's Jorg, from Paris.

He looks tan and fit in his stained lederhosen. He gives me a leering wink and starts working his way around the circle. I'm trying to figure out why he's here, where Finney is, whether I'm in trouble. It doesn't occur to me that you can't have two bottlers working the same crowd until Babouche meets up with Jorg and starts shouting and poking his chest. Duncan's backing up Babouche, fists clenched. Jorg snarls and shoves Babouche out of the way, there's an explosion of coins out of my Panama, Duncan curses and leaps on Jorg's back— a second shimmering burst and people are yelling, scrambling for money and getting trampled, five or six flics in Charles de Gaulle hats are swooping down, Bill's giving me the cut sign across his throat, I'm lunging for our battered hats when they pop into view, stuffing cables and harps into my daypack and scrambling after Bill's green rucksack as he Excuse-me's his way through the back of our crowd. A scatter-ing of young guys with arms around dates and we've broken into the clear, a breeze is tearing at our hats, a circus-smear of spotlights and careening faces as we veer around the corner and the noise is sud-denly fading, we're alone on a back street—bumping shoulders and gasping, tumbling downhill towards the river.

Avignon is history. Long live the open road.

I'm sitting in the window seat facing backwards, sipping one of the Heinekens I brought us from the cafe car. Lost in a grey blur of graded gravel streaming towards the horizon. Fields of shaggy sunflowers, mountains of woodchips, shrinking billboards. Bill's facing me, snoozing—hands laced behind his head, bare feet resting on the seat next to my hip. A six-person cabin to ourselves. Wind buffeting our hair, side-to-side jerks every time we round a curve. Cannes in three hours.

Bill's T-Shirt of the Day: three tyrannosaurs in a jungle clearing gnashing blocky shark-toothed jaws, tearing each other limb from limb. Fires blazing in the palm trees overhead. Caption reads: OLD NEW YORK.

We're both pretty crispy. Too much wind flapping the tent last night. Polished off the fourth bottle of Côtes du Rhône by flashlight before we crashed.

Pen's in my hand, journal's open. Gnawing on the blue cap.

William Lelyveld Grant III.

Telling me a story before he zoned out. You ever been with a black girl? he asks. We were running through "Brown Sugar" and the question came up.

Nah, I said. I mean I've wondered.

Then he starts telling me about Jeenah. Probably never woulda happened if he hadn't been hurting for Charlayne, who'd gone back to Dwayne, which is a whole other story. Anyway, Jeenah: her daddy was actually Irish-Sicilian, a New York cop, but she musta had some Indian in there too because she had the cheekbones. Skin like butterscotch taffy. He met her last summer in Memphis when he was hanging out at Sun Studios buying beer for the guys running the board. She was singing lead with this gospel-thrash band from Austin called Alamo Jesus Leap. The guitar player was the cleanest-cut little white boy you've ever seen—five-feet-five, wearing a black suit and white shirt and looking like Beaver in *Leave It to Beaver*, except when he took leads he'd crank it up and blow. Nothing happening down below—kid could've used some lessons from Keith Richards—but he had all that Van Halen diddlyshit up top. Everybody kept whispering about how he used to play for the Velvet Elevators up in Rhode Island before he came to Texas and found God. Anyway, there was him and some Chinese guy on drums and a hippie Deadhead on bass with a triple-jointed neck. All of them singing this Zeppelin-meets-Pat Boone stuff about Jesus. Meanwhile Bill is hanging with the boys in the same control room where Sam Phillips watched Elvis nail "That's All Right Mama" back in '54, sipping his two dozenth can of Dixie and staring through the window at Jeenah.

She's wearing black tights, red booties, a belted white t-shirt that covers just enough of her butt to make you pass out because there ain't a man alive who can't tell what's goin' on down there. Squeal like an eel. Plus the black hair splashing down her back. And then she'd close her eyes and start singing—her voice wasn't one of those high killer Oh-please-please-baby-fuck-me-Jesus-honey screams like Aretha, it was about two octaves down and sorta husky, like she didn't really know what to do with it, except the way she puckered her orangey-red lips and leaned towards the WHBQ mike with her fists clenched like she was about to swallow the thing made you forget all about whether she could sing. Plus the huge black-and-whites hanging on the walls in there—Elvis with Scotty Moore, Jerry Lee at the piano, Carl Perkins going bald, Johnny Cash looking like a Fifties greaser. Rockabilly hall-of-famers. They're all staring down at her, trying not to drool.

Anyway, one night around four in the morning when the band's been going at it for thirty-six straight hours and everybody's screaming at everybody they take five and head outside with the guys on the board to smoke Angel Dust or pray to Buddha or whatever gospel-thrashers do to chill out. He and this old black nightwatchman named Buddy are the only two still hanging. They're shooting the shit, playing beer-bowl in the control room—buncha empty cans on the carpet with an Astatic JT-30 harp mike for a ball—when Bill suddenly jumps up, grabs his Harmony pawn-shop special, and zips around the corner into the studio. "Rock and rolllllllll!" he hollers, yanking the cable out of White Boy's Gibson L-5 and plugging it into his axe. Flicks the hundred-watt Marshall head from Standby to On, spins Bass, Treble, Presence, and Volume up to ten. The fretboard is humming; any move he makes is *Apocalypse Now*. He tilts back his straw hat and gives Buddy a wink. Babooooom! He's twang-thrashing "Folsom Prison Blues" the way Johnny woulda done it on mushrooms, slamming into "Mystery Train" like Scotty on speed. The drum set across the room starts keeping time—sticks bouncing, falling off the snare. Feedback from hell every time he swivels towards the four-by-twelve stack. He jumps up on a folding chair and starts running through old rock riffs—"Smoke on the Water," "Jumpin' Jack Flash"—at double-time, like a turntable kicked up to 78. Buddy's holding up a Dixie and hollering him on through the window. He's just yanking the groove sideways into a sorta Chuck-Berry-meets-Hendrix thing with his picking palm muting the strings to cut volume—Oh Maybelliiiiine...whah cain't ya be truuue...you mah voodoo chile mama and I wanna make looooove to you—when he looks up and sees Jeenah. She's leaning against the doorway watching him with her arms folded across her titties and her boys hanging on her shoulder like a glam-rock promo shot from Rolling Stone. Those little red booties. Next thing he knows he's leaping down off the chair and kicking into "Blue Suede Shoes" the way he once saw this juke-joint player named Booba Barnes do it at Greene's Lounge downtown—in a raspy old Howlin' Wolf voice—except with little red boots instead of the shoes. You kin knock me out...steal mah car...keep mah likker in an old fruit jar...you kin do anythang that you...want to do...but uh-uh buddy stay offa mah boots...and dontcha...step on mah little red boots.... He's duckwalking towards her as he sings, getting ready to do something so awesomely twisted he hasn't figured it out yet, when he spies her lipstick case on the floor next to the WHBQ mike. Nab! Ultra Persimmon 309 in a .45 caliber shell. He's falling to his knees and playing electric slide with the thing as he inches forward, hollering out a sorta cross between "Hoochie-Coochie Man" and a Levis 501 Jeans commercial. Gypsy woman told mah mothaaaaa...brown sugar tastes so fiiiiine...girlfriend gonna unsnap all your buttons and smear your face with Ultra Pesimmon Three-Oh-Niiiiine.... Closer, closer—she's smiling down at him as he closes in, titties like two softballs she's cradling under her t-shirt. Creamy brown forearms. Bum-ba-boo-ba BUMP! He's loosening his tuning peg, his low E is going down, dowwwwwn, dowwwwwwww-wwn like the sound an editing deck makes when you're rocking the reels trying to find the perfect place to cut and all the words notes and cymbal-crashes are smearing together through the studio monitors into a deep soupy monster-groan—grawwwwrrrrrrrrraunghrrrrrch!—

Then he twangs the sucker and starts tightening. All the way up, until it pops. A hundred watts. He's kneeling at Jeenah's feet, staring her dead in the eyes when she gasps.

Two days later—Sunday afternoon before she flies back to Austin—he's got a date. They're blowing south on Highway 61 in the white '66 Fairlane convertible he borrowed from his roommate Trip, trying to smoke out a backcountry blues jam he's heard about down in the Delta. The car has duel exhausts but one of them fell off right after Trip got it, so the thing sounds sorta aggressive. He's already a little nervous with Jeenah sitting next to him in her tiger-skin jump-suit, long black hair whipping in the breeze. He's heard about the white folks down in Mississippi. Heh heh.

All they've been doing so far back in Memphis is hanging out. Nothing nasty, unless you count looks. They spent one afternoon watching *Jailhouse Rock* and drinking Diet Cokes in her Motel 6 room out on Elvis Presley Boulevard. She thought Elvis looked cute with his greased hair and dark eyes, like the Italian guys she used to date growing up in Greenwich Village. Bill grabbed his guitar when the movie was over and played her "Cadillac Daddy" by Howlin' Wolf with the Willie Johnson part thrash-metallized. Gave her a sorta crash-course in blues. She had no idea about Wolf, Joe Hill Louis, Big Walter Horton—all the black guys Sam Phillips dragged in from the cotton fields and recorded at Sun before Elvis and Carl Perkins stole the show. You see a bunch of white boys on the walls, you figure they're the whole story. Like once you've heard Junior Parker sing "Mystery Train" with the quiver in his voice—it's the difference between a guy who's feeling it and a guy who's putting it on. That's all rock-and-roll was. You can't blame Elvis. If he'd had a hellhound on his trail instead of fifty zillion teenyboppers he probably coulda sung the real stuff. Of course nobody was listening to Robert Johnson back then until Clapton did his heroin time-warp thing with Cream. Jeenah's painting her toenails red, listening. She thinks Clapton would be sexier if he'd move when he sings, like George Michael or Bruce. Bruce! Bill's trying not to puke. Talk about white boys who can't sing the blues. You'd think a black girl would know better. He ain't gonna argue, though. He's half in love already. The burnt-oil smell of her hair— like Charlayne's back home—is making his heart do strange things.

Now it's Sunday afternoon—hot as shit, cicadas ticking in the trees—and they're ten miles south of Memphis, crossing the state line into Mississippi with Charley Patton moaning about boll-weevils on the cassette player. Four lanes squeeze down to two and suddenly they're in farm country, the Seven-Elevens and video stores are gone. Dusty green plants in long rows stretching off to clumps of trees at the horizon. Nobody in the fields except a few guys on tractors. Whenever they pass a shack tilting sideways like a house of cards Bill keeps expecting to see an old black guy in a Panama hat picking his dobro on the back porch, but the places are all boarded up.

They make Clarksdale around two. People stare at Jeenah and him when they push through the screen door into this luncheonette. More at Jeenah's tiger-skin jumpsuit than at him, but there's definitely a weird feeling. You can't tell if it's really there or you're making it up or both. Nobody says anything to them except the waitress. They have a couple of glasses of iced tea each plus the hot tamales and get out. It feels good to be back in Trip's car and moving. He's kinda glad the thing makes so much noise. Fuck these goddamn peckerwood rednecks. He's starting to feel like himself.

The place they're looking for is a guy named Junior Magee's in a town called Alligator, eight miles south of Clarksdale on Highway 61. He heard about it from a black guy he met one night in the alley next to the Peabody Hotel when he was sneaking nips from a pint of Johnny Walker Black before the Albert King show. Trucker's cap, cowboy boots, grimy blue shirt open to the navel, smelled like he'd been working the fields all week. Bill gave him a hit, they started talking blues. Pretty soon they were yelling and slapping and the guy was telling him about the jam at Junior's—how all he had to do was get on down there and drink with the people, share his bottle like he was doing right now and everything would be fine. Show the people you're with 'em. Bill gave him the rest of the scotch and five cigarettes and the guy grabbed his hand and wouldn't let go until Bill promised he'd make the trip.

He tells Jeenah the story as he's hanging a sharp right off the highway, except without the part about the guy's smell. She says Cool. She's wearing dark-green sunglasses with orange plastic frames that match her lipstick. He looks up in the rearview mirror. Mirrored shades with one cracked lens, straw hat jammed tight. State trooper from hell. Y'all in Missuhsippah naaaww, boah, he drawls. She gives him a look over the top of her sunglasses. Don't even try, she says, smile tugging at the corner of her big beautiful mouth.

Oily gravel spits up under the Fairlane as they cruise down this shady back road. Floating over a rise and suddenly they're in business—the road splits right across some railroad tracks, left down a dead-end street lined with buildings on one side. He parks in front of Jones' Store and they get out. The post office is next door:

ALLIGATOR MISSISSIPPI 38720. Next to the post office is a sorta ghost town: three or four rickety grey wood frames from buildings that musta burned down forty years ago, with grass and weeds sprouting up where the floorboards used to be. Crickets skreeking. The kind of place Robert Johnson used to hitchhike to and play for tips in front of. Bill yanks out a stalk of grass and starts chewing. Jeenah's kicking the dust with her red booties. Not a whole hell of a lot going on. Then this young guy pushes out from between bushes at the dead end.

Bill goes Howdy and the guy looks up and says Hi in a soft voice like his mind's on something else. He's wearing an Aquaculture News trucker's cap and a 2 LIVE CREW: NASTY AS THEY WANNA BE t-shirt. Turns out he works at some catfish farm down in Greenville and plays bass in a local disco band. Earth, Wind & Fire, the BeeGee's, Denise LaSalle—whatever the people be askin' for, you know. He's shaking hands with Bill, nodding at Jeenah. When he finds out she's a singer he gives her this side-of-the-mouth smile. You sure you ain't no relation to Donna Summer? She laughs and shakes her head. Her voice sounds speeded-up and white after his.

He can't see why they want to party with the old folks at Junior's but he'll be happy to lead the way. They're slamming doors on Trip's Fairlane, he's firing up his dusty black TransAm. Two cars throttling across the tracks. Robert Johnson's voice on the cassette player wobbles like an Arab praising Allah every time they hit a bump.

A couple of miles out of town the TransAm cuts left onto a dirt road. They bounce into the middle of a cotton field and stop in front of this shack. Rusted Coke signs nailed to tarpaper, one of those mail-order "Home Sweet Home" plaques with burned-in letters hanging over the front door. A couple of haunched cats staring out from under the rusted front fender of a grey Ford truck. The door's dangling open on one hinge and Bill can hear music and shouting the moment he cuts the engine. He grabs his guitar and the shopping bag—two six-packs plus a fifth of Black—out of the back seat and follows Jeenah and the young guy on in.

It takes his eyes a moment to adjust. The heat is worse than outside and it smells like fried chicken and spilled beer. People are lazing in chairs, dancing, shimmying. Lots of Batman t-shirts. That you, Lonnie? somebody yells out and the young guy sorta slides sideways and says Y'all got some company. A loud whistle. The music dies. Lord have mercy, says a man's voice, low. Bill can feel Jeenah stiffen against his shoulder. A whole roomful of black folks is staring at them. This huge guy in blue overalls wearing a straw hat like Bill's heaves himself up out of a chair. Alright Junior, Lonnie says. Junior yanks at his overalls like he's adjusting his underwear from outside. Stares from Jeenah to Bill and back as he waddles up. Murphy! he bellows. What the fuck you been puttin' in my whisky? The place explodes. Guys are falling off chairs. Then Bill drops his guitar, pulls the six-packs and fifth out of the shopping bag and says something about folks up in Memphis telling him this was the place for blues. Now I *know* the Devil done took my behind! Junior roars and the place sounds like it's gonna blow sky-high.

Well, they have quite a party. He's never been made to feel so at home. One old lady makes him take a paper plate heaped with fried chicken, potato salad, macaroni salad, and greens; the guy everybody calls Murphy—caved-in cheekbone, pencil mustache—throws an arm around his shoulder, hauls him into the back room, and hands him a Skippy jar with a coupla inches of cloudy lemonade. Shit tastes like worn-out paint thinner mixed with fermented hangovers. The two guys sitting next to Murphy on the bed crack up and slap hands when he chokes. Hell you mean you ain't never tasted no corn liquor? Murphy yells. Cracker boy like you? Shit.

There's a band playing in the front room: big brown-skinned guy thumb-picking electric guitar through an old TV set, young guy with a brown plastic leg—wearing shorts, so you can see the bolts—playing harmonica, bouncy little guy with a white beard drumming on an upside-down cardboard box with a pair of sawed-off broomsticks. A couple of guys are lazing on the sofa staring at a baseball game on TV, even though blues is the only thing coming out of the speaker. The drummer keeps barking Hey! Hey! Hey! and making faces. Bill and Jeenah tap toes while they're eating. One guy on the sofa is giving her the fisheye. She slides closer to Bill; her breath makes him jump every time she whispers in his ear.

Things get wild later on, when they make him play. The booze has sorta pushed him past the point of optimal coordination. Petie—the guitar-player—hands him the cable for his axe; everybody's staring and waiting. This drunk guy with beer-breath and a fishing cap smashed down on his head keeps leaning in singing Whoa baabyyy... you don't haaaaave to gooooo. Bill starts comping behind him and the moment the drummer gets it people are clapping. It turns into a thirteen-and-a-half bar singalong with nobody coming in on the same beat. The first time Bill throws in one of his Robert Johnson licks people holler Yeah baby! and slap hands like he's their discovery and they own him.

Of course Jeenah's got to do a couple. She's sorta reluctant—blues isn't her thing, she's only been singing out for a year and a half—but you can't tell these people no. Not when you look the way she does in tiger skin. Murphy's pouring rounds from his jug, getting folks stoked for the big kickoff. She and Bill finally break huddle and hit with "Summertime." Her voice is a little wobbly, harp player's in the wrong key. The place goes apeshit. Miss Tina Turner, y'all! the drummer shouts. Miss Tina Turner! She's hugging herself and blushing when it's over, giving Bill a look like he saved her ass. They can't lose after that—he swings her through "Moondance" and "Rockin' Robin," she backs him up with go-go's on "Johnny B. Goode." Folks are dancing steps white people couldn't think up in a thousand years. Then Petie borrows his axe and hollers out "Good Mornin' Little Schoolgirl" with knock-on-wood moves in the breaks—slaps, thumps, pitter-patters—like the guitar's barking out words. Bill's just sitting there, soaking it all in. Jeenah leans forward after a while, puts her hand on his knee and whispers Thanks. Her angel lips are so close he can see the tiny black hairs. Oily mist on her flared nose. Her eyes say You can kiss me if you want but he's suddenly too shy. Weird as it sounds.

The Coast

Frayzhjuice. Sahnrahffayelle. Meeramahhhr.

Sank me newt ah Kahn. Lifting my eyes from the page as the voice crackles in my ears, losing myself in sheeted azure rimmed with beige crust. Summer breeze blowing through windows as we slow. Like every Caribbean afternoon you've never tasted. Limbs stretching in salt water. Shiver me timbers.

Glancing back down. Thirty pages filled; ten days and counting. I'm slapping it shut. The spine's so mangled the pen barely fits.

Yo Bill, I say.

No answer. Mouth lolling open, snores. Smelly bare feet on the seat next to my hip.

That's allll-riiiiiiight, I drawl. I can uuuuuuuuse you.

Nothing.

I reach down between my legs, shove my journal in my daypack, pull out a harp. Play reveille. Freely, with blues inflections.

He groans.

Wake-up call, I say.

He cracks open one eye, fixes it on me. You ain't nothing but a dream anyhow, he says.

Four-and-a-half minutes to Cannes, I say, jumping up and stepping over his legs.

I'm packed, he says, stretching and yawning.

I heave my pack down off the overhead rack, lay it flat across two seats, loop one nylon strap around each end of my daypack, cinch tight. You were dead to the world, I grunt as I hoist it onto my back.

He's lazing back like he owns the train. Just getting ready for the weekend, he chuckles.

Twenty minutes later we're standing on the hotel reservations line at the Office du Tourisme—Bill has his guitar out, working on double-time rockabilly strums—when I hear a familiar voice go After you, ladies. I turn around. Joey Cohen is holding the glass door open for two blondes with light-blue packs. The clean white smile, the sunburned schnoz. Mr. Rockville Centah, Lawn-GUY-lint. Leather wineskin looped across his huge chest like a cartridge belt, t-shirt reading KISS ME, I'M SPANISH. The black eye is new.

Yo Joey, I call out.

He looks up, does a double-take. Holy shit, he says. Points at me and snaps his fingers a couple of times. From Avignon.

McKay, I say.

McKay man, he says, limping towards me. How the fuck are you?

I thought you and Michel were in Barcelona, I say as we grab hands.

He makes a face. Some bullshit started going down, man, I'm like whoa, lemme get back to a place I'm gonna be abused by foreigners I can halfway deal with.

We're goin' on a holidaaaaay now, Bill booms as he kicks his rucksacked Mouse forward in line. Gonna take a villa or a small chalayyyyy....

Joey eyes him warily.

This is Bill, I say. We met up after you guys left.

Bill gives him a cowboy nod, shows teeth. Hah.

Howyoudoin', Joey grunts.

Bill drops his jawbone. Welllllll...one for the money...two for the show...three to get ready now go cat go.... He spins away from the line, strumming.

Joey squints up at me, jerks his head. You know this guy?

He's cool, I say. I nudge my Mouse with my toe. We've been working together.

Hey, that's right. How'd that shit with the harmonica ever—

Oh oh oh, I interrupt, I tracked down that swimming pool you told me about.

His eyes twinkle. You know about this place, right?

I'm smiling. The whole beach.

He elbows me in the ribs. Is Europe a party or what, man?

Bill twists to a stop, draws himself upright, clasps his guitar to his heart. What is best in laaahhhhhf? he drawls, finger raised like a Baptist preacher. Ah will tell yew: Tuh crush yer enemies, see them driven before you, and hear the lamentation of their women.

Joey's smile fades, then blossoms. Conan the Barbarian, he says.

Bill yanks off his mirrored shades. His eyes are gleaming. Heh heh heh.

This guy's fucking out there, man, Joey laughs, eyes crinkling.

You should see him when he's been drinking, I say.

The Magic Dick note on my A-harp is shot. I discover this when I'm warming up after the picnic we've just had in our new pensione room high in the hills overlooking town. Joey's doing pushups next to the queen-sized bed; Bill's shower-singing. I slide up to the ten hole blow and mash down hard. A dead, airy sound. I snatch a jeweler's file out of my daypack and pry off the metal cover plate. The reed looks okay. Hairline gap, no congealed spit. I flex it gently with the tip of the file. Still no note. I probe again, flexing and releasing, massaging the tiny brass strip. Droplets of spit curl around it when I blow. Nothing.

I carefully replace the cover plate, then hurl the harp at the floor, leap after it and stomp it flat with the heel of my running shoe. Joey rolls into a tensed crouch; I pick it up and toss it out the window.

You gotta kill 'em when they die, I say, snatching his wineskin off the corner of the bathroom door and squirting myself a mouthful.

Joey runs a hand back through his brown curls. Yo man, next time spare me the heart attack.

Got mah diddy-wah-diddy... Bill croons from the bathroom. That's mah diddy-wah-diddy...oh somebody please tell me what diddy-wah-diddy means....

I slide over to my pack, bury my arm up to the hilt, come back out with a fistful of white plastic cases. Ah, preparedness. My new A glints when I cup it. Tang of freshly-minted nickel, varnished pine comb. The sound's too dry—my yelps and howls don't speak. I grab our vin-de-table bottle off the dresser and stalk into the bathroom. Bill's writhing behind the curtain, wrestling with the snake.

Take out ya false teeth, mama, I drawl, I wanna sssssuck on yo' gums. I slosh red wine down through all ten holes, wrist-flick it into the sink. The stuff splatters like blood.

Waaaaaaaugh! Bill roars, parting the curtains and nailing me from crotch-height.

Shit! I yell, leaping back and dropping the bottle on the tile floor. It explodes.

Joey sticks his head through. Look at this shit, he says disgustedly.

I stare at the broken glass, splattered wine, water. Bill's chuckling and la-de-dahing behind the curtain. The comb of my harp is stained reddish-purple. Little sucker sounds like a caged hyena—raucous, hungry, bouncing off the walls.

Joey tells us about Barcelona as we're strolling down through town towards the beach. He knows we're probably looking at his black eye and thinking The guy's a total animal, but it wasn't like that. The Spanish people are cool. Very emotional, but hey: he's no saint himself. Just your typically average American guy who likes to party, etcetera. Plus he has a Puerto Rican lady back home on Long Island, so he's like Mister No-Attitude about the whole Hispanic thing. He figures he and Michel are gonna have a wild fucking blowout. Little does he know.

The first couple of days down there are pretty mellow. He's hanging with Michel and the Canucks—that's what they call each other, even though one of them is actually a Maltese from Ecuador or some shit. Go figure. Anyway, it's him and Michel and the three Canucks at this rooming house called the Hostal, run by this semi-retarded little dwarf who keeps limping around the place wiping off tables with a wet rag and going Fiesta! Arriba! American Express! Smiling at everybody, posing for pictures with the girls like the munchkin on *Love Boat*. The guy's a total trip. Everybody calls him

Jose. The only thing wrong with the place is having to share one shower with about fifty other guys. Mornings are like Forget about it. Jose's running around, dishing out scrambled eggs, banging on the bathroom door yelling Fiesta! Arriba! American Express!, you got about five hundred naked guys staggering around with towels falling off their buns and hangovers muttering Suck my cock Jose and trying to remember where they threw their clothes the night before.

Basically it's like Spring Break down in Florida: lie on the beach all day, check out local pussy, drink a few beers to cool off, then go out and get shitfaced at night. Everybody drinks this dark Guinessy Spanish brew called Voldam, or else red wine. Vino rojo. The wine-skin scene is fucked up because guys at the Hostal are always getting into fights and going apeshit, ruining people's clothes, etcetera. Some assholes have no self-control, man. He's glad this big Geman Brunhilda-type finally got pissed off and took some American guy out. Boom! She musta been on steroids. Jose posed for a picture sitting on her shoulder.

So they have a couple of mellow beach days and then the third day comes along and it's raining. Whaddya gonna do? He's not big on museums and all the typical tourist shit. He and the Canucks end up catching some Bruce Lee triple feature with Spanish dubbed in, which is almost as weird as eating in one of those Cuban-Chinese places back in New York when the waiter starts cursing out the cook. Everybody screaming Die motherfucker! in the wrong language. After the flicks they grab dinner at a McDonald's across the street— America is everywhere, man, you can't get away—and head over to the Barrio Chino, otherwise known as the red-light district. Not much in the way of hookers. Mostly video-games places and Indian guys selling Hustler, your basic Times Square scene. He blows thirty pesetas on a t-shirt to prove he made it this far south.

They end up—we're talking third or fourth move of the night—at a bullfighters' bar called Il Toro. You can tell it's for bullfighters because the walls are covered with swords and hats and capes, pictures of famous matadors, bulls' heads mounted with the horns sticking out like at a hunting lodge. Great decor. Within about ten minutes he and the Canucks start talking to these three Spanish dudes sitting at the next table. Bluejeans, white t-shirts, smoking Marlboros. The moment he opens his mouth they're giving him high fives and calling him Rocky. The Canucks they could care less about—they're just totally into the whole American thing. Trying out their vocabulary. Coca-cola! Michael Jackson! Ozone Park! One of the guys has a cousin who spent a summer in Queens. This other guy named Gitanillo starts buying him drinks—this weird green shit called absinthe that drips through a strainer into water and turns brown. Tastes like bitter licorice. They crack up when he makes faces. Slap him on the shoulder.

He has a couple of those. He's starting to get seriously fucked up. He and Gitanillo—it turns out the guy is like the hottest young bullfighter in Barcelona. Joey's like Yeah, right when the guy first starts pointing at the pictures on the walls and saying I do that shit. His English is lousy; the Canucks are translating. Then Gitanillo waves his hand, says I show you and stands up. Lifts his t-shirt up to his neck. Scars like you wouldn't believe. Joey just sits there going Holy shit. The guy pulls down his shirt and they start having this unbelievable rap about bulls and swords and banderillos and samurai warriors—Joey's been into the whole Eastern thing ever since he started taking karate, he's busting a nut trying to explain the difference between the katana or fighting sword and the five-inch wakizashi you use when it's time to commit seppuku. Gitanillo's looking pretty lost, so Joey pulls out his Swiss Army knife and makes like he's slitting left to right across his guts and twisting upward. Gitanillo makes a face like Whoa and waves his hand. This one is no good, he says. Muerte. Rocky is dead. Everybody cracks up, somebody slaps Joey on the back. He's feeling like Man, this is what you get for trying to talk about important shit with retards. He keeps his cool and has another drink.

By the time he's put down Licorice From Hell Numero Fiveo they've pushed back the tables—he's crouching at one end of the bar with his fingers behind his ears, Gitanillo's standing in the middle of the room snapping a red napkin like a cape with the Canucks and everybody else going berserk. He's figuring like, You guys wanna laugh at my ass, let's not dick around. First couple of times he charges it's all a big game—he aims for the napkin, Gitanillo pulls it away, he keeps going a few more feet, slows to a stop, looks around like Whoa, what's going on here? Everybody shouts Ole! Then he figures he'll make it interesting. Throw in a couple of karate moves. This time he waits until the last second, hooks his arm out—boom!—and catches Gitanillo around the neck. Nothing: empty air. All he sees is a flash as the guy ducks. He knows his leg is fucked the moment he hits the floor. He gets up—everybody is laughing, he's brushing himself off and trying to act like it's all a big joke, part of him wants to walk over to the skinny brown dickhead and get stupid. This other part is like Yo Joey man, lighten up. He takes a deep breath. The bartender is this hot-looking Spanish chick—dark hair, about twenty, eyes so brown they're almost black. If her hair were curly she could be cousins with his lady back home. He smiles and grabs his crotch. Hey babe, he calls out. How's life? The bitch totally ignores him. He limps towards the bar, still smiling. What's the matter? he says. Don't you talk to Americans? He's being super-friendly. Next thing he knows he's jumping up on a chair, dropping his pants, giving her a full view.

How was he supposed to know she was the guy's sister? Once these Latinos get excited it's like Forget about it. The first couple of times Gitanillo popped him he was like Hey man, don't make me hurt you. Pushing him away, trying to grab his hands. Then the guy hit him in the face and he went off. Pow! He kept expecting a rumble but everybody just stood there. The third time Gitanillo got up off the floor Joey was like I know when I'm not wanted, get me outta here. The guy's sister was screaming. Michel pulled him away. No fucking idea how he got home. The Canucks were gone when Jose dragged him down off his bunk at ten-thirty this morning. Nah, he just met Michel back in Avignon. No big deal. He was getting itchy to move on anyway.

Across the boulevard, through the palm trees, past the bouf-fanted matron walking her fluffy white Pekingese, out onto the Promenade de la Croissette. The bay is spread out in front of us— Ti-D-Bowl blue, fading to pale green as it laps at the beach. The sand is littered with bare breasts, brown-nippled and gleaming in the after-noon glare. Shoulders, bellies. I follow Bill over to the railing. He leaps up on his upended Mouse, hugs his guitar. Scans the landscape.

Shee-it, he murmurs.

Right? Joey agrees, giving the word a little lift.

The sun grazes my face. Warm salty breeze. There's a Spanish galleon moored at the end of a long pier on our right. A forest of white masts heaving like sea-urchin spines. I glance at my watch. Still Friday.

I can't believe I'm supposed to be in Bologna in like sixty-four hours, I say.

Whaddya, got plans? Joey grunts, tilting forward against the railing to stretch his calves.

A friend I'm supposed to meet.

Those three down there? Bill says, pointing. I'll bet they're from some little town about.... He pauses, squints, tilts his head. Thirty-five miles outside of Stockholm.

Joey glances up. On the purple towels?

I'll bet they rub noses in the winter and drink glooooog.

I'm in love, I say.

You'll get over it, Joey sighs, straightening up.

I wish they all could bebebebe California giiiiiiirls, Bill sings, turning the last word into a punk sneer as he slam-dances with his guitar case.

Later, sprawled on my towel with my toes wriggling into the sand, I'm the first to smell smoke. I lift my head. A grey cloud is billowing upward—slowly, gently, relentlessly—from the hills over-looking town. I watch it spread towards the sun. A girl on my left screams and doubles over as her boyfriend grabs her from behind, then giggles. Falls to her knees in the sand. They start kissing tenderly, stroking faces. The air reminds me of Vermont in January with all the woodstoves spewing. Tangy. I jab Joey with my elbow.

Yo man, check it out.

What's up? he grunts without moving.

Poontang alert.

He rolls onto his elbow, squints groggily. Black welt under his eye.

I lied, I say.

Fuck you, he groans, falling back.

Nuclear winter.

He snorts. Nuclear winter.

Look up in the sky, man.

He opens his eyes, tilts his head back on the sand. Breaks into a grin. Hey Bill man, check this shit out.

Bill is stretched out like a Mexican on siesta—straw hat shading his face, legs crossed at the ankles. Empty black dress shoes side by side on the sand. Silence.

Bill, Joey barks.

He mumbles into his hat without moving.

Get a look at the lunar eclipse, man.

Solar, I murmur.

Bill pushes his hat away just as the smoke-cloud slides across the sun. The light on the beach suddenly gets weird and cool, lemony-velvet. Murmurs on all sides.

Woooowwwww, Bill drawls, naively and sarcastically.

Joey's chuckling as he stretches. Fucking Riviera, man. I want my money back.

I stare at the dull glowing ball. I've always liked the smell of wood smoke, when I'm in ski country. Flecks of papery white ash are falling out of the sky.

y seven that evening the air is so bad my eyes are stinging. The sun is flirting with the horizon, there's a bruised purple band stretching from the hills above town far out to sea. The bay is rum-colored and glittery. We've sucked Joey's wineskin dry, we're the last holdouts on the beach—Bill is hollering sea shanties at a couple of fascinated seagulls, Joey is sliding around in the sand practicing his samurai moves with a piece of driftwood, I'm working myself into a controlled frenzy trying to shave down the swollen wooden comb of my A-harp with the smaller blade of my Swiss Army knife. This needs to be done so the bulging nubs won't scrape my lips raw. Wine, beer, seawater—the liquids I've poured in there have turned the reed-dividers into a buzz saw. Monstrously funky sound, but your skin can only take so much. I'm squinting, paring, trying to precision engineer. My hand slips, the blade digs too deep; a little diamond-shaped hunk of pine breaks off between holes six and seven. Bill hears me cursing and comes over. He takes a look, scratches his head. Wowwwww, he says, sympathizing. He tells me I really oughta not sweat it quite so much. He's seen old black guys play blues on harps way more damaged than that. I tell him where he can go. He grins in the evilest way. You know what a gentleman is? he asks. Fuck you, I mutter. A gentleman, he says, is somebody who *could* play the harmonica but doesn't. I stare at him. He's holding his finger up. Who said that? I ask. He grins. His grin shoots straight through me and makes me feel crazy. Ah did, he drawls. Guitar dangling from the piece of clothesline around his neck. He grabs the thing with both hands and snaps off an insanely ferocious ten-second lead up at the twelfth fret. Whammer Jammer lemme hear ya, Dickie! he yells, whapping the chord we always kick off with. What can I do? The man owns my heart. I hit the soaring high note; the seagulls scatter. We're back in gear.

The smoke, it turns out, is the fault of a forest fire up in the hills. That's what a young Frenchwoman in a BEST MONTANA: PROFESSIONAL BRONX SURFER t-shirt tells us when we're buying Heinekens from her kiosk up on the Promenade. She waves her hand in disgust; we can see what the smoke's doing to business. Not a promising night for the Bottom Stompers. We sip beer and wander down the boardwalk. Joey's wearing my hat—experimenting with various tilts, trying for the Bogey look. Bill's playing slide with the Heineken can and crying Heyyyyyaayeaaaahhhh at nobody in particular. I'm grooving, floating, swinging my Mouse. It feels good to be walking barefoot on warm concrete at sundown with the Mediterranean swishing on the sand to my right, even if the breeze does smell like mesquite-grilled seaweed. The grand hotels—Carlton, Gray D'Albion, Majestic—loom over the palm trees to my left, beaded with pearl-strings of light.

We're getting ready to retreat for more booze when we hear an air-raid siren up ahead. A crowd materializing where stairs come up from the beach. We knock back our beers and pull in. A tall young black guy in a tux—beige skin, tight bleached blond curls, black-rimmed glasses with one lens missing—is standing at attention, face panicked as he salutes an invisible superior. There's a boombox on the ground behind him with speakers spread, a white cardboard sign with dripping red letters: DR. LIVINGSTONE, DIRECT FROM LONDON. The siren rises to fever pitch, his raised hand starts to tremble, the tremors spread down his arm and out through his body until his teeth are chattering, his glasses are falling off, he's about to self-destruct. POOF! The siren cuts out, the Blue Danube Waltz is playing and he's smiling beatifically as he begins a slow-motion walk. Each body part seems to float as he lifts it, suspended in ether. He lowers his eyes, gazes dreamily at his hand. Wiggles his fingers. Marvelous! He smiles blissfully, opens his mouth—his face is suddenly blanching, his chest heaving as his eyes roll upward and cheeks puff, he's touching fingers to his lips, struggling not to vomit as the sound of someone retching bubbles up through the waltz. ZAP! We've snapped back to real time, the Pink Panther theme is playing and he's Mr. Suave as he eases smoothly through the crowd, strides towards an older couple—blue blazer on the guy, diamonds on the woman—and offers them cigarettes from the pack he's just slipped out of his tux pocket. They glance at him and keep walking. He throws back his head, laughs and makes cocktail-party chatter with the space where they were. Throws his head back further, laughs harder. Brays, roars—the funhouse soundtrack has suddenly gone psycho, his grin is a lock-jawed leer, his head is snapping like a yanked hunk of puppet wood, his neck is about to break when BLADABLADABLADABLADABLADA!—his head suddenly whips from side to side. Crashes and explosions, like a munitions dump tumbling downstairs. His jaw is slack, tongue lolling; he's a kicked puppy waiting for the next blow. ZAP! *Been a long time since I rock and rolllllled!* screams the soundtrack and he's springing to life, hip-hopping towards the low wall separating the boardwalk from the beach. He spins, rises to his full height and beams. *We read that you were killed five different times in five different places,* he mouths, holding up a finger. *Yes, and it was true every single tuh-tuh-tuh-tuh-time.* He pivots as the word blossoms into a beat-box track and begins to dance—jerkily, like a robot, then more fluidly, dropping into a flying split and leaping up, spinning in circles. He strips off his jacket and lays it on the wall. He's wearing a white t-shirt speckled with fine print. His face is contorted with rage—Malcolm X at the podium—as he points at his chest and mouths each word snarling out of the box:

> I am black. I was born black.
> When I go out in the sun, I am black.
> When I am sick, I am still black.
> When I am dying, I am black.
> When they bury me, I am still black.
>
> You are white. You were born pink.
> When you go out in the sun, you turn brown.
> When you are sick, you turn white.
> When you are dying, you go grey.
> When they bury you, you are purple.

AND YOU'VE GOT THE FUCKING NERVE TO CALL ME COLOURED!

ZAP! The jungle beat has evaporated, "The Stripper" is playing—he's hugging his arms, batting his eyelashes. A trombone growls; his snake-tongue flickers. He rakes his eyes across the crowd. Slips his hand under his t-shirt, caresses his belly and chest. Groans. Lifts his shirt up over his face, ripples his abdominals, then pulls it off and tosses it on the ground. His shoes are next: one black, one brown. White socks. He licks his lips, grabs his crotch, reaches for his belt, unbuckles it. His pants fall. He steps out. Six-and-a-half feet of butterscotch limbs draped in white boxer shorts. His eyes flash with venom. He screws up his face, clenches his fist. *I'll get you my pretty!* the box cackles. *AND YOUR LITTLE DOG TOO! NYAHAHAHA!* He dances a jig, spins, scoops up the broomstick next to his prop bag, vaults up onto the concrete wall, shoves it between his legs—theme song of the Wicked Witch is playing—and leaps off.

The crowd goes crazy. Kids are yelling and scrambling after him, pouring down the steps as he rockets across the sand. Seagulls scatter. He plows into the surf, staggers, leaps with arms outstretched. The sky and sea open out behind him like apricot layer-cake laced with rum. War-whoops as he bursts through and whirls to face the beach. I'm free! he shouts in his own voice, holding the broomstick up like a scepter. He has an English accent. Don't you see, goddammit? You're terrified of me because I'm *free!*

Bill knows him from Paris, it turns out: they hung with Finney, tripped, got hauled in by the flics after scandalizing the Beaubourg and ended up partying with a couple of Moroccan transvestites from the Bois de Boulogne. He smells of cheap aftershave and has a tan billy-goat tuft, like a jazz trumpeter. Gives Bill a big kiss on the cheek; Bill goes Aw shucks. Then he pulls on his slacks and spins away to pass the hat.

We play right after that. Bill breaks a string as we're tuning up—rummages in his case, pulls out a half-finished pint of Johnny Walker Black he'd forgotten about since Milan. The first gulp makes me shiver. I was put on this planet to torture sweet swinging sobs out of small brass reeds. I grab the bottle and kill it. Next thing I know I'm leaping onto my upended Mouse—barefoot, poised, smoky salt air caressing my thighs. The Mediterranean is at my back. Joey's grinning up at me; he's gonna bodyguard when our female fans get rowdy. My heart falters. Who *is* this guy I've become? Then I take a deep breath—fire racing through my veins—and blow.

A long, seamless, angular, swaying glide of a jam. Dogs yapping in backyards, roosters shrieking, vintage Corvette with a blown head-gasket. Remember that high school hike alone up into Harriman Park? Blue flame roaring on the Svea stove—stew pocketa-pocking, spattering, hot. The stillness afterwards. Brook burbling over rocks. You sighed in the morning when you woke and smelled woods.

Set's over before I know it. Joey handing me my Panama after he's emptied it into Bill's case. Fucking awesome, man. Bill slapping my back. I'm lost in space. Kneeling to unplug, save my batteries. Who is that chunky blonde? Aviator glasses, white singlet. Eyeing me all night. Do I want to go for a walk? Forward, edgy, young. Breasts swelling together as she leans down to talk. She's smiling. I'm gone.

In the morning I wake early from a dream I can't remember and lie in bed shivering, even though sun is already slanting through the open window and it's obviously going to be a blistering beach day. Joey's snoring next to me in the bed we drew straws for, face crumpled in his pillow; Bill's snoozing in the cot. Dr. Livingstone's slouched in the chair by the door, where I tripped over him when I came in. My eyes unfocus on his bleached blond Afro. Forty-eight hours to connect with Paul in Bologna. I slip out of bed, pad over to my pack, rummage feverishly. A sweet musty smell, like dirty socks bathed in cologne. Gamy refolded t-shirts, a baggie filled with wild apricot pulp. Hardcover original edition of Edmund Wilson's *Europe Without Baedecker,* which I haven't glanced at once. That guy back in New York must have been high. I pull out the train schedule, snatch my journal pen and slip into the bathroom. Slivers of broken wine bottle prick my toes as I rotate and sit, flip pages. Europe according to Eurrail is numbered black dots on a computer-generated map. Cannes is a stretch of blank white coastline between Marseille 95 and Nice 105. Flipping, scanning. Nice-to...Nice-to-Bologna trains do not exist. Another northern Italian terminus? Milano Centrale.

Nice-to-Milano Centrale trains exist. Begin with what exists. Control is key. Rationality. Relinquish rationality and chaos reigns.

When I've figured everything out I stand up, wipe, smell my own shit, wipe with six more huge wads of leathery brown tissue—dampened alternating with dry—and flush the whole mess. Wash hands, slap my face. Bill goes Hah when I come out—he's thrown back the sheet, a boyish body in blue bikini briefs with ankles crossed, hands laced—but I can't talk now, I have to run and clear my head. No joke. Stripping off underpants, pulling on shorts and a singlet, my Nikes are knotted and I'm out the door.

Cannes in early morning is a fifteen-year-old girl tossing her hair in the breeze blowing through the window of a June school bus. I float down out of the hills and out onto the Promenade. Palm fronds fluttering, an Arab in tan chinos raking butts off a stretch of hotel beach. Heart murmurs from five hours' sleep. Swerving right, past the park bench where Nicole and I necked—laser-green grass, lilies so orange and new they look fake. No trace of last night's smoke.

I shouldn't push the pace so soon but I can't hold back. Flushing out accumulated poisons. Salt in your sweat's the dead give-away. Sailboat hulls bumping softly as I blur by, masts bobbing and weaving, dizzying whiffs of brine. *Berkeley Review* piece on Kerouac's nuclear-age prosodics will be out when you get home. Hemingway grinding out *The Sun Also Rises*—one long burst between *Toronto Star* cables. Fishing with Mike in Basque country. It felt good to be warm and in bed.

I'm flopping to a stop as the sidewalk tails off, face to face with a tiny dusty purple flower, gasping. Tell me about warm and in bed. Tell me about nipples swelling large and brown, silky black hair sweeping down across shoulders, ache in her liquid eyes as you cradle each other—hips fusing, an endless streaming plunge. Tell me about five years. Catching my breath as the flower suddenly wobbles, blurs. Throat ripped and aching, scattered across the sky. Tell me how free you feel now.

Whirling, head up, arms and legs pumping as I slap away tears and fly back. What does not destroy me. Veering across the road as a crimson Renault swoops down, blares. Cool morning smell of damp scrubbed stones in the shade of an old marketplace. Easing off a hair; my heart's redlining, struggling to catch up. Lungs bursting with dry heat as I dart back onto the Promenade and rise onto my toes. What about that Nicole Chouinard from Tannersville, Nova Scotia? Only nineteen years old, hey. I hafta smile as I flop to a stop. You sleazy fucking decadent-ass cradle-robbing slime-dog. Ah yes. You will survive. Take a deep breath, walk it off. Fall onto this lush grass under these palm trees. Panting, spent, eyes unfocusing into depthless blue as my brain freewheels, unreels. There's more day to dawn. Too much ain't enough. It don't mean a thing if it ain't got that swing. Stinging as they fill; I'm almost blind.

We make a regular t-shirt army that morning, heading down through town after baguettes and cafe creme at the pensione. Joey's wearing a Tasmanian-Devil-goes-French model—black beret, pointed mustaches, bulging eyes—with the slobbered proposal VOULEZ-VOUS COUCHEZ AVEC MOI? Bill's has a poem: ROSES ARE RED, ORCHIDS ARE BLACK, I LOVE YOU BEST WHEN YOU LIE ON YOUR BACK. Delightfully tacky, according to Dr. Livingstone; his reads I KNOW YOU ARE, BUT WHAT AM

I? Mine's borrowed from Bill, a blown-up repro of an ad from the Village Voice:

IGUANAS

Small $29.95, w/kit - $69.95. Med. Iguana and our
Exclusive Iguana Chow also avail. Call Today &
Receive Your Iguana Tomorrow. 1-800-932-9335.

Bill actually tries to call the number from a phone booth on Rue Carnot—makes me stand still so he can read it, asks me if we should go for small or medium. Receiver crooked as he feeds francs into slots. I tell him he must be high. Naaaaaah, he drawls. The doctor's before-breakfast hash is making time flow like mellow oil. Sunlight sheeting onto my bare arms. Bill clears his throat, winks. Starts to chat with his invisible phone-mate. The voice of a born con—rich, folksy, ripe with the promise of deals to be struck, killings to be made. Any possibility of shipping overseas? Might as well throw in an extra bag of chow for the little fella. Dr. Livingstone is doubled over, hysterical, screaming No! in a stage-whisper. Bill hangs up; the coin-return rattles like he's hit cherries at Vegas. He scoops the jackpot back into his chinos and slides away—rucksacked Mouse swinging, straw hat flopping shredded edges. If ah don't go craaaaay-zyyyy, he booms, ah will surely lose mah miiiiiiind....

We blow into a Felix Potin for picnicstuffs. Stocky women with steel-rimmed glasses stare fiercely as we tilt through the aisles, packs bumping. *Vin rouge* is a buck a bottle; we each grab a big one. Hunks of brie, bags of carrots, fragrant peaches. Back into the street—Joey's brandishing his baguette as he expounds on samurai philosophy. The warrior's sword is his soul, his duty is to serve, his way is found in death. Dr. Livingstone licks his lips. Will Joey be his love-slave? Geddoudda heah, Joey sneers, boffing him. Ah got a meeeeean red spidahhhh, Bill bellows. She's webbin' allll ovah towwwwwn....

Roaring onto the boardwalk, tumbling down the steps, plowing into the sand. Ta chirps the doctor, veering off. The beach is a velvety beige blanket checkered with sprawling nippled womanflesh. Which way to jump? We drop packs and Mouses between two luxuriously be-thighed sets of nymphs. Theory is we'll soak up the scene until midafternoon, then hike to the train station and hop a Nice express. Theory begins to crumble with the first salt whiff. I'm stripping down to my trunks, hotfooting past oiled torsos, plunging into the surf. Floating in the Mediterranean womb. A moment of transcendental clarity as I rise fresh-limbed from the sea. Flopping belly-first onto my towel, lost in trickling salty terrycloth cool-cradling my hidden face. Tap on my shoulder: Nicole self-consciously chunky in a white bikini, eyes veiled by teardrop glasses. Heloooo, she murmurs. Found ya, hey. Pecks me on the lips. Her breath smells like Juicy-Fruit gum.

Within ten minutes her breasts are bared—I'm trying not to stare—and she's telling me she's felt bad all night because she lied, she's not really nineteen, hey, only seventeen. Will I still be her pen pal for life? Of course, I mumble, elbows propped. Reptilian stirrings under the rock of my hips. Sweat misting her upper lip as she stretches out next to me, lower breast pillowing against the sand. Aureoles the size of large brown birthmarks. Salty dew glistening in her navel.

We lie back and bake side by side. Sun seeping into my blood; I'm a snake on a sandbar, drugged. All is illusion. Murmur of the noontide sea.

Time passes. Heads are lifted, eyes rubbed. Lunch: I'm tearing off a hunk of Joey's baguette, smearing ripe brie. Ammoniac tang of sweaty sneaker socks. Swiss Army knife flipped open, bottle clamped between my knees. Snock! We're alternating glugs—Nicole explaining why she missed spring term in school; something to do with the scars on her wrists. Everything okay now. She writes poems. Would I read them if she sent them? Sure, I'm murmuring. Welllll the girl you looooove don't treat you right sometiiiiiime, Bill hollers, whapping his Harmony like he means it. Evil-dawg grin, eyes twinkling into mine as he grabs our bottle and swigs. Next thing I know—powerless to say no—I'm saying I'll be back and scampering after him.

Her name's Caroline; they're Tarzan and Friday. American and two English hanging out on the concrete walkway between the end of the Promenade and the lighthouse. Bill tips his hat; her chipped-tooth grin is a dazzler. Small full breasts under a grey U.S. FOOTBALL singlet. Lots of tan leg. Suddenly we're five, sharing a bottle and a joint, gazing down at a blue yacht moored just below. MAXIME'S A LA MER. Party in progress—guys in blue blazers, dolls in careless dresses.

Ih gaw innis mawning, Tarzan sneers, chameleon popeyes bulging. 'Ay've been fookin tanking ih up aow daye. We trawyed to geh in. 'Ay said we nayded cravats, saw we puh awn cravats. Jerking his chin at the tie-dyed silk scarf around Friday's neck. Buh 'ay stiw wooh-int leh us in. Fookin wanks.

They're from the East End, London. She's from Seattle but not for a long time. Thin gold chain around one ankle; dusty bare feet. Grey-blue eyes that land glancingly. Used to produce jazz concerts—Nice, Antibes—but her boss is away in Paris, she hasn't been paid, suitcase got ripped off last week.

Hi babes, she says, kissing the cheek of a black guy in a flowered shirt who nods as he slips past us, murmurs, No problem with a French accent, flashes her a wicked grin over his shoulder, disappears into the hold of a large white sailboat at pier's end. HYPERION, ST. KITTS.

Bill hands me the roach Tarzan just handed him. Red-faced, veins throbbing. Slaps his hat on Caroline's head and lets out an explosive heyaaaaahahaha! People on the MAXIME'S deck glance up.

They'll stone you when you're riding in your caaaaaar, he sneer-bellows, windmill-strumming towards the gangplank. They'll stone you when you're playing your guitaaaaaaar.... I would not be so all aloooooone...EVERYBODY MUST GET STONED!

He's up on the brushed aluminum guardrails—legs laced, hollering, weaving violently—when I notice three flics on the Promenade breaking into a trot.

Bill, I bark, flicking the roach away. I'm barefoot, shirtless, unshaven, smell like hemp.

No answer. The guy's having a fit.

They slow to a fast walk as they file onto the walkway. Charles de Gaulle caps, dark-blue epaulets with stars.

Ring arouna raowsie, Tarzan mutters.

Bill doesn't see a thing until they're on top of him—clustered at knee-height, arms folded. His eyes open; he stops singing. A fortyish woman in a backless dress on board MAXIME'S applauds with hands raised, shouts Bravo!

Flic with the mustache glances at his assistants, back at Bill.

Bob Deeylan, he says dryly.

The wildness in Bill's eyes falters, then flames into a melting grin. Naaaaaw, he drawls, Dylan can't sing. Hell, I was just....

La musique est fini, monsieur.

I mean I'm real sorry if I.... Shee-it. Shaking his head as he hops down off the guardrail. Y'all wanna see some sorta I.D.? American passport? Glancing from man to man as he reaches into his back pocket.

Head flic holds up his hand. No more music. Compris? You go now. Glances at us. Everybody. Make my day.

Other two flics smile like this is a private joke. They watch as we hop down onto the beach. Friday staggers, drops the bottle. Tarzan hoots and springs; Caroline takes his hand. The sand is blazing, heavy with heat, a lumpy trampoline that doesn't bounce. Bill jostles me with his shoulder as we land. I'm down for the count, laughing so hard I can hardly breathe.

Party of the summer is that night, on a tiny island—clump of rocks fifty feet square—just off the curled right claw of Cannes bay. Bring your own whatever. Everybody's invited; Dr. Livingstone gives us directions.

We head down at seven after freshening up at the pensione, where we surprise our concierge by showing up at five-thirty asking for the room we just vacated that morning. Nice didn't happen, we explain. Tomorrow. She gives us a severe look, hands us keys. Bathroom has been mopped. Fresh towels, clean sheets.

Bill's T-shirt of the Night: I'VE TALKED TURKEY WITH EDDIE SALTER CALLS; picture of Yosemite Sam about to blow away Tweetie Bird with a double-barreled shotgun. Joey's wearing his Gold's muscle-shirt, I'm recycling my PINE BARRENS MARATHON singlet. Purple nylon smells like it's been galloped through the Western States Hundred-Miler with no water stops. My shoulders are the color of rare prime rib. Maintain or die.

Spoon-clinks on saucers as we veer past evening cafes—sugar cubes stirred into espresso-foam, thickening and shining. JENLAIN A PRESSION.

Tumbling along the Promenade behind Bill's rucksacked Mouse; he's all teeth, eyesparkle, and guitar-strums nodding at every girl we pass singing Yeah...you're gonna look so cute...Sunglasses and a bathing suit...Wontcha be the baby of my dreams...like the pretty ladies in the magaziiiiines....

Out towards the lighthouse—the boardwalk opens up—and left onto the gravel spit. There's the doctor, vogueing on his rock pile. Three, four, five girls waving us across. Fifty feet of open water.

My Reeboks are off, knotted, tossed over my shoulder as I step in. Five-foot-wide concrete slab covered with greenish slime to the touch. Water swirling around my calves. Currents are tricky; balance is key. Hold your Mouse high, out of spray's way.

Smashing! he's crying, hauling me up. House-music thumping out of the boombox perched behind him. She's the same as youuuuu and meeeee but she's homeless...homeless...just singing to herself... lah-dah-DEE lah-dah-DAH...lah-dah-DEE lah-dah-DAH....

Leslie and Blake from Hollins College, Virginia. Sandy from Vancouver wearing Tretorns with nice calves. Bottle thrust into my hand as I clamber to high ground, set my Mouse in a crevasse. Tides gurgling through stony mazes down below.

Tanya and Riike from Stuttgart. U.S. Army pea jackets, short bleached blond hair like otter fur. Samir—Moroccan, collegiate, gleaming brown eyes—is wearing a faded blue work shirt by Brooklyn Sportswear. Patch on his breast reads:

Oceanic Steamship
EXTRA BLUE
The Best Way

To Understand
The Authentic
Boarding Crews
Rugged Briny Life

I'm sitting on a rock glugging bottoms-up red inhaling salty sparkling angled sun watching Dr. Livingstone massage the shoulders of a tan white girl in a yellow sundress. Breaking off a hunk of passing me thanks smeared baguette with creamy goat white splashed cheese down with wine. Heaven at last.

Crash of glass breaking behind me, tinkling down between rocks. Joey whoooooing. Fuckin Samir better get it under control, man.

Who is this creature walking on water? Snaky black tresses tumbling down across shoulders as she picks her way towards us, staggers, catches herself, mutters softly, glides forward, grabs hold, scampers up. White t-shirt tucked into black shorts. Feast of curves.

Later: sharing my dusk falling bottle. Lips murmuring Dolores in my close ear. She cries when Elvees dies. Only a girl in Sao Paolo, they playing his sexy movies after school. Boyfriend is gypsy. Cannes today; tomorrow, who knows? Gaita means harmonica when I'm pulling mine out and Waaaaaaugh!

Can she try? I'm Of course. She's cupping it to her hidden lips. Fingers cradling nursing suckling. Our eyes lock. Crouching in the rainforest at the dawn of time, haunch to haunch. Like this? Toot.

Her grin—I'm giggling, we're both—is a throb-arching crotch of embarrassed dark eyes. Never leave this island. Everybody disappear and we'll be ache-singing happy forever.

Stars hurled across my head-tilting night. There's the Big Dipper. Tidefingers reaching for me through splashing rocks down below.

Heyyyyyy a veering Bill-holler of teeth-breath on my neck. Staring up into my mirrored eyes and his sharp-angled straw hat. Ya wanna get some sorta jam-thing goin'? Strumming his axe.

No I

Yesyesyes Dolores whispering little girl eyes disbelieving delighted.

Ca maaaaaaahn.

Shit I don't maybe a little

Ah got raaaaamblin'...ah got raaaaamblin' awwwwn mah miiiiiiind.... He's all teeth flashing lips twisted button-nose rocking back on one leg, snapping forward, pulling at my deepest sigh. Reaching down to strangle that bitch note. Well I haaaates tuh leave yah baaaaaybaaaah but ya treeeeeeaaaats me soooo unkiiiiiind....

Dr. Livingstone's hashpipe floating from hand to hand, ember glowing dull red as I'm pulling sweet fumes curling down into my tendrils tickling wrapping tightening glowing red as I pull and hold. Roaring inside my there. Loosening all ties, springs are sprung sproinged sprangletoothed slapdragons of sufferin succota—

Ah got mean thiiiiings...mean things alllll awwwwn mah miiiiiiind....

Teeth clanking harp-metal smoke cupped between my hands. Aaaaaaoooooo! Dolores is melting happy-teeth pouring browneyes into my heart.

Shouts across the water as we look up, Dr. Livingstone waving Hel-lo darling! Small humped shadow picking its way through the soft night, struggling against currents. Flashlight traps a flail of sunburned limbs clambering. I'm Oh shit not again as she towards me.

Go back. Want to find home. Tidefingers slurping, reaching for your Mouse through dark cracked rocks.

Runnin' dowwwwwn to the staaaaation...catch the first mail-train ah—

Orange lily stuck behind her stringy blonde hair fingers massaging my frozen burned shoulders like a piece of meat she thinks she owns.

Found ya, hey? Breath tickling into my neck.

Ice caves, palaces, flesh cracking into crystals, shattering, hard as diamond. Leave alone.

Joey winking like he knows what I'm feeling.

Dolores nibbling a fingernail try to smiling.

Dr. Livingstone hovering behind Bill—fingers looped around the fretboard, helping him jerk off his axe.

Splash! down below and I'm shivering harp's jammed in my lurching pocket as I bumping Nicole staggering to hook my Mouse up out of the crevasse. Gotta go. Getting dark out there.

Stick stuck in a hornet's nest, Dolores a wobbling smear of No. You must be playing some more.

Nobody tells me what I—

Cowboy nod from Bill's veering leer drawling Ah got the bluuuues about mah baaaaabyyyyyy...and my baaaabyyyyy got the bluuuuues about meeeeeee....

Tearing away—juices dripping, cables dangling, Mouse yanking my arm socket as I'm careening towards the slurping black. Most yourself now. Toes scraping against rocks clears fog. Aim for the blinking red lighthouse jiggles as I crouch, take deep breaths, step down into swirling cool-sucking my shins up to the knee-joint.

Joey's Yo douchebagging clattering on behind me rocks.

Letting go as I slide away. Slipperslime against bare feet. Other side—dry gravel—is only fifteen yards away. Tugging at my calves in a sudden swirling, trying to steady, hugging my Mouse to the thumping black blood-knot as I'm falling, screaming No! cannon-balling in.

B ill helps me perform major surgery in our pensione room the next morning. All I have is my Swiss Army knife; he pulls pliers out of his guitar case. Unscrews four bolts and the black wire mesh with the logo—a squatting black rodent—comes off. The speaker cone is splotched with salt, smells like mildewed newspaper. We work our fingernails under the steel frame and pry it away from the sound hole. The magnet is fist sized and very heavy; there's a small transformer bolted across two struts, twined yellow and blue wires snaking like an umbilical cord to the printed circuit board under the control panel. Two chunky black burglar-alarm batteries bolted down with a block of raw pine. Classic American design.

The bathtub seems like the best place to drain fluids. We ease across the room, connected by wires; I'm cradling the speaker, Bill's trying not to slosh. All we gotta do is dryer out, he murmurs. She gonna be jes fiiiine. We're leaning over the tub, struggling for the best pour-angle, when my finger slips and punches through the damp paper cone. Summer is officially over.

My curses rouse Joey. What the fuck's goin' on in there? he groans. Bill tries to calm me down by pointing out that the old blues guys used to rip holes in their speakers intentionally to get that raw sound. Hell, he says, that's what Ike Turner did on "Rocket 88." She'll really bark now. I'm crying inside; if I had a shotgun I would load for bear and splatter small animals.

Petit dejeuner downstairs is the same old shit—stale crusts, greasy butter, runny jam, bitter coffee froth. I stuff my face and feel dizzy and hollow. Bill agrees with me about the need for scrambled with sausage, homefries and toast. Best breakfast he had passing through New York was from this sourpussed old black lady at the Hudson View Diner on 125th Street, next to the river. Yes ma'am, he kept mumbling—she'd slap the menu down, tap her foot, scribble his order, snatch it back, yell something racist at the Mexican cook, say the coldest damn thing to some old black guy in white meatpacking clothes smeared with blood sitting at the counter who was trying to flirt with her. Coffee? she'd bark, glaring over her shoulder. Yes ma'am. Clatter, spill, mutter. Here you go, baby—sweet all of a sudden, like she was his grandmother. Real American food. He grabbed a toothpick next to the register when he was through, left her a big tip, pushed through the front door, jogged across the access road. The river was right there—grey-green, ripply, smelled like ocean breezes and crankcase sludge from the cars guys were working on upwind. He musta thought up three new songs that morning, leaning on the railing and picking his teeth, looking up at the George Washington Bridge.

Joey's toweling his hair dry when we get back. Gotta catch a train to Morocco—he and Samir are blood brothers now, he was like Whoa when the guy took out his switchblade at the end of the party, the whole Arab thing sort of spooked him even though they'd been drinking from the same jug all night. Not to mention AIDS, except this guy was a major lech when it came to babes so he wasn't worried about pretty-boy shit. Then he figured What the fuck and just did it. Go for the red. The guy was hugging him, etcetera. Gave him the address of some house in Marrakech where his mother lives with his three sisters, said You must come, you must stay, give them this note, tell them I send you, they treat you like a prince. Whaddya gonna do? Yabba-dabba-doo.

I reassemble my Mouse after I've packed—an hour on the windowsill has dried things out—and plug in. A sickly low hum. Bill's not worried; all she needs is a couple of new batteries and you'll be honking. Worse comes to worse you can always call 'Lectrosonics out in Albuquerque and have them two-day express the shit. He strips off his I'VE TALKED TURKEY WITH EDDIE SALTER CALLS shirt, folds it with three quick snaps, flips open his guitar case, heaves out his axe, snatches a fresh t-shirt off the stack underneath, lays the folded one on top, and scoops a thigamajig out of the spare-strings compartment. Hands it to me. Two inputs with volume controls on each, quarter-inch phone jack sticking out the back. He's humming as he wriggles into his clean shirt. For your Mouse, I murmur. Might be a little crowded, he says, but we'll make it. He tucks in, gives me the old devil grin; plastered across his chest are a leering skull and a six-story apartment building in flames. BROOKLYN: WHERE THE WEAK ARE KILLED AND EATEN. Heeeeyaaaahhhhh! he whoops. Git ready.

Things are rushed later, at the train station. Joey uses international hand language, persuades a mop-pusher in a blue smock to snap a Three Musketeers picture before we split up. His arm stings around my sunburned neck; Bill and I are on the outside—hats tilted, feet perched on Mice. Cheese! He takes back his camera, thanks the guy in halting Arabic. Better practice the shit now, man, I'm gonna need it.

We trade addresses, promise to keep in touch. His black eye has faded to purplish-yellow. He gives us bearhugs as his train pulls even with the platform. I'm leaning down awkwardly. His biceps bulge next to my chin; he smells squeaky-clean, like deodorant soap. Yo man, it was real. He lets go, pivots, hauls himself up and on. Bill and I wave when he finds a window seat and gives us a thumbs-up. He looks happy.

Well ah cain't get yew off of mah mind...
When ah try ah'm jes' waistin' mah time...
Well ah've tried an' ah've tried...an' all night lawng ah've cried....
Well ah cain't get yew off of mah mind....

We're moving again. No empty seats in the six-person compartment—Sunday on the Riviera—so we're lounging in the aisle, drinking beer and jamming, wahooing into the wind. Coldest Kronenbourgs of the summer; Bill bought four through the window from a sandwich-cart guy on our quai. Buried in crushed ice. Twenty-four hours and counting.

We make Antibes and fall off. Beach seems like the best place to freshen up before busking; we grab a loaf of peasant bread from a coin-op machine—Bill has wine and cheese from the party—and swing down through town. Signs keep urging us towards Le Musee Picasso. Grey castle on a hill through fluttering olive branches. Next thing I know we're in a cool high-ceilinged room staring at a huge stone sculpture of a woman's head. All nose and jaw, skewed eyes. Bill snickers; he used to catch fish like that downriver from the nuke plant in Cape Girardeau, growing up. On the wall is a large painting of satyrs—horse below, man above—tooting on panpipes as a woman dances a jig. She has tiny cartoon features, huge breasts with skewed nipples.

The beach is almost deserted. Bill opens the red wine as we're tearing off clothes and we glug. The water is warm and delicious; I splash back out of the foam, freshly skinned. Creamy white goat's cheese, bread torn off with saltwater teeth trickling. Blowfish-prickle when I stroke my jaw; haven't shaved since Paris. The wine is tart and good.

On the way back into town we come up behind a guy hauling a black Gretch case and collapsible luggage carrier piled with a Doobie amp, battery pack, dented mike shoved through a harmonica holder and immobilized with fifty rubber bands. COWGIRLS NEED LOVE TOO t-shirt with sleeves cut off; tattoos with arrows sticking through hearts. He notices our Mice and asks. Stuyve from Liverpool. Bristly brown mustache, reddened lips. Steel-blue eyes that look like they could hypnotize deer.

Five minutes later we're three in a bar, junk piles at our feet. Stuyve's old lady has gone back to Paris. Ever heard of Genvieve Bersault? Third-highest paid model in France. Wipes his nose. Been drinking all day; already put down fifteen liters of this piss. Had a fight with her last night—so many beer piquants he was walking home like this: wiggles hand to show staggering. Stewed as a newt. Cops came as he was washing up. Told the bitch she had ten minutes to pack and get out. Runs hand back through hair, laughs. Left her for two months once. Bloody Jesus. Do we know anything about Frog politics? Took up with a girl—dad was number two in the Ministry of Defense. Not much to look at; big girl. Rich. Laughs. Half a million francs when they took up; five thousand overdraft when he left. Bought him three cars. Rabbit and two Triumphs. Blew up all three—engines seized. Gulps beer, wipes his mustache.

Working tomorrow; gent downtown asked if he'd act in a movie. Three birds, hour-and-a-half, three thousand. Of course the old lady was green. Glances at his watch. Supposed to ring him by two if she got in okay. Knows he's here. If that phone rings it's probably for him. The phone rings twice, both times for the young Moroccan with beeper playing Pac-Man by the open door. Stuyve finally lurches to his feet; one low-cut black suede Beatles boot is unzipped. Terraces are a piss but we might as well.

Sunlight raking across dazed eyes as we clutter back onto the sidewalk, shoulders jostling. My Mouse is dead weight. Stuyve leads the way, head low, crooning to nobody:

> Now you're lookin' at a man that's gittin' kinda mad...
> I've had lotsa luck but it's all been bad...
> No matter how I struggle and striiiive...
> I'll never get out of this world alive...

We hear the Peruvians before we see them—old familiar thump-and-whistle, like a coca-stoked fife-and-drum band. Rounding a corner and there they are, serenading cafe-sitters in front of a dry fountain. Inca noses, fedoras. Four Mouses plus the hide of a hairy beast lashed around a hollow log. Girl selling their tape is small, husky, dark, has a face like a rough-cut jewel. White teeth when people toss change in the ukulele case at her feet.

We stagger, stop, stare. Stuyve curses under his breath. They've nicked my spot, the fucking wogs. Flushed red lips. I glance at Bill; he's toeing the cobblestones, silent behind mirrored shades.

Stuyve staggers over, unzips his fly, cuts loose into the ukulele case; the girl screams; the five Indians drop instruments and rush him, dance back as he lifts and sprays wildly, then close in as he trickles dry; he grabs the closest by the shoulders and gives him a vicious head-butt, sending him sprawling. Come on! he snarls, daring all comers. Come on! They pounce—his dick is dangling—and spread-eagle him on the ground, one per limb. Go home and live in the fucking trees where you belong! he screams, writhing like a sacrifice about to happen. Girl's cradling the wounded guy, sobbing; cafe-sitters are staring.

I stand there, pack biting into my shoulders. Peruvians aren't doing a thing to Stuyve except holding him down.

Maybe we oughta split, Bill murmurs.

Hear that lonesome whipporwill...
He sounds too blue to fly...
The midnight train is winding low...
I'm so lonesome I could cry....

We're on the train to Nice, riding shotgun in the waiting area at car's end—hollering, crazed, howling at each other's goofs. The latest wine bottle is empty; every rounded curve staggers us. Bill's cracked mirrored lens has shattered and fallen out—his guitar case whapped him as we were leaping on—but he's wearing the shades anyway. One naked pirate eye.

He reaches a crotch hand into his chinos and comes out with a tiny plastic bag. Two shriveled lumps crowned with dusky purple caps. He's amazed when I ask. I don't do that shit, I murmur, breathless. Naaaaah, he grins. Kerouac woulda jumped at the...sheeit. Ya gotta live it if ya wanna write it. He quotes Blake, Aldous Huxley, the Drug Enforcement Administration. One puny little cowflop fungus won't kill me. Half of one. Field research.

The train sways, glides, veers. I've never been shamed by peer pressure into doing something stupid. Always taken great pride in my independence of mind.

One-quarter, I counter.

He's leering as he fingers one out of the baggie.

Bill, I say.

He pops it in his mouth, swallows, sticks the second between his molars, and bears down. Hands me a chunk of the purple cap. I stare at it. Italy tomorrow morning. I bite off half—it tastes like stale moldy cork—and swallow, hand him the rest as I grab the wine bottle and rinse.

Wimp! he yells, gobbling it and snatching the bottle back.

Druggie! I cough.

Aaaaaah, he sighs, belching softly.

They call themselves the Leapin' Hoovers. Four-piece rockabilly combo from Cambridge, England, plus the cute skinny girl on washboard. Our paths cross in the Zone Pietonne after we've wandered down from the Nice train station. I'm not feeling anything from the mushrooms; Bill keeps dropping his jawbone and twang-booming some line about how his dog died yesterday. Dawg. Except the faintest edge of strobe-delay when I move my head too fast.

They're jumping around, working the crowd. Tall young guy on bass has Popeye tattoos and dangling cigarette lips. Spins the thing like a top between slaps. T-shirt reads PLAY IT SAFE, PLAY IT COOL—WEAR A JIFFI ON YOUR TOOL.

Guys on guitar and trap set could be twins. Freckles, jumbled rat teeth, scraped knees below baggy shorts.

Kid up front sings badly, blows harp worse. Grins like an early Beatle: freshness, innocence. Every song is about vacuum cleaners. Rock Around The Hoover, Got My Hoover Working. Leaps into a handstand in front of the bass player—loops his legs over the guy's shoulders, blows an upside-down solo before introducing the band.

Getting a bit hectic.

All four have thick shiny hair billowing back like matching tidal waves. Black & White Pomade. Lead singer Jimmy shows me the jar after their set. Like scented bear grease. Same stuff Elvis used.

Fancy a bit of wine? Passing it around.

Guitarist Thorney is letting Bill check out his Gretch Nashville. Bill's Harmony is out of the case—flipped over into Thorney's hands to show place names scratched into varnish. Twenty or thirty, plus the bumper sticker: EXUBERANCE IS BEAUTY.

Fine by me. If it's okay with the fellas. Bassist Mickey is sucking smoke, flipping his butt away, exhaling. Nods all round.

The Leapin' Bottom Stompin' Hoovers.

Bill plugs me in. Sound's sour. I'm flat from him. Sharp? Finger stuck in my ear as I blow octaves. Nothing lines up.

I said shake...rattle...and HOOVER!

We're jamming—snare and cymbals clattering miles behind me, Mickey humming bass-lines offstage left. Bill's Mouse spewing our shapeless roar. Makes up his own lyrics—babbling like an eye-patched auctioneer as he duckwalks in front of Thorney, rises onto toes, stiffens, jerks, wrenches the strangled neck.

Whyn't you fuck off, mate?

Jostling Thorney with his moves—once, twice—and suddenly Thorney's growling and shoving him, he's pitching forward, staggering, putting hands out as he falls. Crack of splintered wood.

Thorney! Jimmy halting the band with a raised hand.

No really, I'm serious—he's ruining the fucking—

Bill lies still, spread-eagled. Slowly picks himself up. Nobody says a word. The neck is bent, ripped partway from the body.

Look, Jimmy murmurs, we're all terribly—

Bill lifts the thing off, raises it overhead—Thorney ducks—and smashes it against the cobblestones. Staggers as he yanks the pickup out from between spaghettied strings, then stomps the rest. Bumper sticker holds the sounding board together; the gouged place names finally disintegrate in a pile of kindling.

He's all teeth as he faces Thorney—finger pointing, shades skewed. You're dead, he pants. It may take a while.

By the time we find our way back to Gare Nice-Ville that night—sky dark, dusty bottle of Cuervo Gold we've bought half-gone—Bill is crowing about how much lighter his guitar case is with only the t-shirts and blanket roll. He's beating out Afro-thrash conga lines on the thing, I'm slinging tequila and vocalizing; Nice is a carousel-smear of cafes and Chinese restaurants lining Avenue Jean-Medecin. Overnight train at eleven; Milan by dawn. Twelve more hours.

The station is rippling with anticipation and yells. Every American college kid within two hundred miles seems to have descended. Tangerine copies of *Let's Go Europe* and *Lonely Planet*, rolled up straw mats lashed to backpacks, panicked girls in hiking shorts juggling plastic torpedo-bottles of Evian. We careen past newsstands towards our idling train; dozens of guys wearing Wayfarers are hanging out of open windows like grinning lizards, hollering us on.

All the couchettes have been snapped up. We find an empty six-person compartment, heave packs into luggage racks. When I get back from the toilet Bill is lounging with his shades off, feet up; two blondes with tan legs glance up nervously from the window seats. I stroke my grizzled jaw and throw myself into the seat opposite Bill. He's grinning at me, stretching arms overhead. Looks like we'll be spending the night together. Heh heh.

A short, stocky older man in a grey suit, clerical collar, spectacles pokes his head in, then enters and sits. Black briefcase, copy of a book: *Les Juifs, Les Chretiens, et Rome du Unieme Siecle*. He nods, I nod. Fellow scholars. Yep, Bill chuckles. Suddenly his guitar case is in his lap, he's tapping out a Delta shuffle humming Meeee and the devil...was walkin' side bah side...I'm gonna beeeeat mah womaaaan 'till ah get satisfiiiiied.... Blondes are staring; I nod in time, offer them a hit of Cuervo—they shake heads—then swig and pass it to Bill. They're from Sweden, heading to Verona. Offer us toasted wheat crackers and nectarines. Juice dripping down my chin; when I come back from the toilet a second time the priest is gone. A steam whistle hoots, our seats jerk. Cheers from next door as we start rolling.

One of the blondes falls asleep after Bill and I jam awhile, other stares out the window, bored. The train sways and rocks. We finish our tequila, pull down shades, turn off lights, slide seatbacks and cushions down so they join in the middle to make a lawn-like expanse for sleeping. Bill stretches out next to the turned back of the drowsy blonde, my back's facing him. The moment my head touches down everything whirls. The train is a centrifuge trying to separate me into component parts. Some fanged alien is trying to claw its way out of my intestines. A whole nest. I lurch into the hall and veer into the WC, slide the bolt, fall to my knees, stare at the roaring hole. Faint tarry breeze. Something raging inside me wants out. Please dear God. Endless straining gargle; sweat bursting onto my face, cooling me. Ammoniac sting in my nostrils as I blow, wipe snot away. Shit in my pants.

I clean off, gulp water from the sink and hobble back. Bill mumbles when I slide open the door; dark humid air smelling of dirty socks and fruit. Crumpling onto my stretch of cushion. The aliens have pitchforks and are dancing around a fire. This time when I lurch aisle-ward I take my sweater for a pillow.

I spend many miles in the WC. The floor is convenient. We creak to a stop more than once. Voices singsonging down below, by the tracks. Updraft through the potty hole when we're moving. I crawl back to the cabin sometime before dawn. Purple-black skies; wind clattering through open windows, empty hallways.

Porter bangs on our door at six-thirty. Bill scratches his head, dozes; he's staying on until Venice. Blondes can sleep for another hour. I heave my pack down, jam my filthy sweater under the flap, grab my hat and Mouse. Yo Bill, I murmur. He stirs but doesn't wake. Hair whorled, mouth open, hugging himself. I already have his folks' address back home. He looks boyish. Somebody's kid brother. Peaceful. I reach out a hand towards his shoulder, then stop, heave on my pack, and ease quietly into the hall.

Milano Centrale is a cavernous aircraft hangar—velvety grey light sifting down through dusty glass—and gibberish is the native tongue. I stumble past a cappuccino stand; men in short-sleeved shirts eye my Mouse as they toss back liquids, wipe mouths. Destinations flutter and reform on the computerized Treni in Partenzi board. Time sags. I'm dozing aboard a midmorning shuttle to Bologna. Facing me are three young Canadians with crewcuts and rattails. Dennis programs computers for the Mounties; repairs Game Boys in his spare time, hey. Rocking gently, shooting on ball bearings down an endless straightaway. Stewing in my own smells.

Bologna is one more grey slate platform I stumble down onto through retractable doors that seize my pack frame like jaws. *Let's Go* clutched discreetly; four numbered pensiones starred with Paul's blue felt-tip. I'm standing before a greying bearded man in the Ufficia Informazione di Turistica. Phone cradled; manager of Pensione #1 squawking in his ear. He glances at me. Paul Goldberg was staying at this place three days before he leaves since one day and does not pay. Do I know perhaps where he goes?

I think about this. Foaming at the mouth seems like a reasonable response but I don't have enough spit.

Is not good, he clucks, hanging up. Non e buono. He squints at *Let's Go*, telephones Pensione #2, glances at his fingernails. Babbles crisply when someone comes on. Eccola? Benissimo. Smiling as he hangs up; will show me on a map.

Dragging my hollow carcass down endless grey streets. Senegalese vendors hawking Tom Cruise videos: *Top Gun, Risky Business, Color Of Money*. I used to be clean-shaven like that. Pensione Marconi engraved in gold on black marble as I heave open a door, trudge up steps.

Lady at the front desk—short, stocky, loose mass of greying black hair tied back—is happy to see me. Oh ho. Hands waving, voice rising: perhaps I can tell her where Signor Goldberg is? Goes out early this morning, owes now two days rent. She speaks no English but the gist is clear: I am in the land of Grand Opera. She dislikes my hat; I am a strange unclean vagabond. Why do Americans plague her like this?

I stand before her, pack freighting my shoulders, a shivering wreck. Lost.

Alorra! she cries, looking past me.

Hey captain, a voice calls out, and I turn to see him crossing the threshold. Beard, droopy glasses, thinning hair.

Paul! I cry.

I can explain everything, he says. Then, blanching: What on earth happened to *you*?

To Florence With Paul

First thing he does is throw me in the shower. Our room has a shower, a minor miracle. Viva Italia.

Scalding water rakes my shoulders; I yelp, jump back, jockey gearshifts until the rain is lukewarm, a drenching balm. Then stand dumbly and let it flood. I have become death. Waterfingers tearing me limb from limb, scattering my bones across the sea.

He sticks his hand through the curtain with soap and shampoo. Aussie Papaya with Bioflavanoids and Kerotin; silhouetted red kangaroo jack-rabbiting across the setting sun. Smells like orange juice concentrate, oozes like cum. There is a God and his name is lather.

Are we having fun yet? he calls out.

I groan.

I thought that's what you said.

I'm gonna shave after my nap, I splutter, rinsing.

I meant to ask.

I'd probably slit my throat if I tried now.

Here's your towel, he says, perching it on the stall corner.

Merci.

Prego.

He's sitting on the bed when I step out, head buried in a book. The room has a clean cool feel with the blinds down, tile floors.

That's our bed, huh? I say, padding towards my pack.

'Tis indeed.

How romantic. I struggle with the knot, flip back the flap, drop my reeking sweater on the floor. Cheaper than a double, right?

Much.

A diesel bus wheezes down below. His hair and beard are backlit like a corona from the bedside light.

Watcha reading? I ask, dropping my towel as I pull on clean underwear.

He holds it up without looking at me. *The Divine Comedy*.

He shrugs. I figure we're making a pilgrimage to the man's hometown, I might as well brush up.

I pull on Bill's Iguana shirt—cleanest thing I have—and lower myself gently onto the bed, groaning. My shoulders have been scoured by blowtorches.

Are you quite alright? he says dryly, turning and peering down at me over the bridge of his glasses.

Solarcaine, I moan weakly.

Roast, he hisses, in the fires of hell.

He screams in mock-terror when I grab him. The smell of his underarms is familiar and strong. Our tussle ends when he bops me over the head with his book.

Back, he cackles. Back. Begone.

Oooooh shit, I chuckle as I fall back. Then, when my shoulders hit: Aaaaaaah!

You happen to be in luck, he says, heaving himself off the bed. He walks over to the sink, rummages in his toilet kit, tosses me a plastic bottle filled with clear green goop. Nivea Aloe Vera.

Aaaaaay, I say.

Kenna was convinced I'd be incinerated by the Florentine sun.

The mink from Montreal, I hoot, stripping off my shirt. Now this shit I wanna hear about.

After your nap.

Can I hijack you for a minute?

His fingers dab at my shoulders—cool, slippery, fastidious—and every touch soothes.

So much for Band-Aids on broken legs. He snaps shut the cap. What *have* you been doing for the past week?

I collapse on my belly and groan.

He's chuckling as he clicks off the reading light. Have a good one.

Lights blossoms from the hall, fades, vanishes with a click. I pull back the covers and ease under. The pillowcase feels clean and cool against my cheek in the dark room. A motorcycle buzzes by down below. Monday afternoon in Bologna. Hugging my pillow, stretching my limbs between cool sheets. Crotch pushing into the mattress. I wonder how Helen is. Tonight makes two weeks.

I was sitting at my desk in New York—a Monday night on the May/June cusp—outlining a new essay: "Hardboiled or Free-Blown: Hemingway, Kerouac, and the Struggle for Postwar American Prose." I had my summer's work cut out for me. Helen and her old Cornell crew-buddy Caroline, meanwhile, were muscling box after box out the front door of our apartment and down through the lobby into Caroline's Volvo wagon.

I wasn't having much luck. The ideas were there but my mind kept wandering. Trial separation was the phrase we'd been using. Three months to figure out how we felt.

I didn't hear her come in. She murmured my name; I looked up. She smiled weakly, brushed a few stray hairs out of her face with the back of her gardening glove.

"Hiya," I said.

The corner of her mouth twitched. "I just thought I'd let you know we only have one load left. We, um...." She paused, eyes on the floor.

"Almost done, huh?"

"A couple of boxes."

"Cool."

"I thought Caroline and I would drop off this load and then I'd come back and, ah...."

"Say bye bye until September."

She hesitated, eyes glittering, then turned and disappeared down the hall. I heard the front door slam with a muffled metallic thump.

I sat for a moment, motionless. Then I wrenched myself to my feet and swung out through the doorway.

Her study was halfway down the hall. I paused when I reached it. Two cardboard boxes and a brown gooseneck lamp were sitting in the middle of the bare wood floor. Everything else had vanished. Her swivel-backed chair, her black metal desk, the pink-and-green Matisse poster of dancing maenads. *The New Yorker* cartoons of decrepit pit bulls staring at bare light bulbs she'd cut out and hung at strategic points around the room. Her clothes. The shelves were still there—sunken into the wall—but her clothes had magically disappeared. I walked over to the bare shelves and ran my hand across the flat white paint. Her nightgowns and slips and the pair of blue silk panties I'd given her one Valentine's Day. The woven wicker basket that held her bras with the buried calico sachet. I leaned down and sniffed. You could still smell faint traces of perfume, lavendery and astringent.

I turned around. Her desk lamp was resting in the triangular space between the angled boxes. The cord was coiled and knotted, the way it always is on new lamps. I fell to my knees next to the closer box, prying open cardboard flaps and rummaging inside. Dozens of legal-sized manila folders, neatly stacked. I undid the string on the top folder and flipped it open. Old letters—dozens and dozens, each in its own ripped envelope. I pulled one out. My own handwriting stared back at me: Mlle Helen Solomon, Auberge des Etudiennes, 128 Rue de la Source, 75008 Paris, FRANCE. Nine months' worth of five-year-old love letters. A lot of good they'd done. I shoved the envelope back and re-looped. Whatever I was looking for wasn't in the first box anyway, just a bunch of old college exams and ten years' worth of cancelled checks. I pushed through to the bottom, shoved it aside and moved on. The flaps of the second box flew open; I sat on my haunches staring down at a slim maroon folder crowning a stack of papers. Her journal.

I hesitated, then picked it up, slipped off the rubber band and started paging through. The first entry was written in red ink—obviously one of those times we'd had a fight and she'd run off to her study and slammed the door, you could tell how upset she was by how distended her handwriting was, she was crying as she wrote, spewing her heart across the page. She always did love to get worked up when she wrote about her own feelings. I flipped the first few pages over when I'd had enough and moved on.

I kept flipping and skimming until a letter caught my eye. Dear Lonnie, it began. Three-quarters of a page, dated a couple of weeks earlier. A quick read. When I finished I put it and her journal on the corner of the open box and leaned against the wall, gazing down through the window into the darkness of our little courtyard.

It wasn't what you'd call a love letter. It was half-finished and left nothing to the imagination. She was very clear about the things she wanted to do to him and vice versa. Most of them were things we'd been doing for years. A few were things I'd have been happy to do if she'd bothered to suggest them. One or two were things I couldn't do because I didn't have a mustache. The letter had never been mailed. She didn't need to mail it now. This was her first night in her new place.

I was still standing by the window when she pushed through the front door. I heard it slam. I heard her walk down the hall and pause. I gave her a moment to absorb the situation. When I turned to see how she was doing her face had fallen most of the way. I snatched up the letter.

"What the hell is this?"

She stared at me, arms dangling, face pale. "You had no right to go in there."

I laughed. "I had no right? Oh man, that's great. That's really great." I shook my head. "'Dear Lonnie, You don't know—you can't know—how badly I want you inside me. I ache when I think of our last kiss, your beautiful blond mustache and the softness of your—'"

"Give me that," she hissed.

"Get out," I said softly.

"Give me the letter."

"Get OUT!" I shouted, slamming it down. I slapped the folder into the box, heaved it into my arms and lurched towards the doorway. "Get OUT!" I screamed as she pulled back. I barged through and swung left, propped the box on my knee when I reached the front door, yanked it open, slammed the box onto the landing, swung back into her study, heaved the second box into my arms, grabbed the lamp, swung down the hall and out the door, slammed the second box onto the landing, threw the lamp at the box, and swung down the hall towards her study. We almost collided as she came out.

"Get OUT!" I roared, spinning and following her. Her black hair was bouncing on her shoulders. Her butt was jiggling under her shorts. She said nothing. She walked out without looking back. I slammed the door as hard as I could. I was hoping it would disintegrate but it only made a loud noise. I could hear her struggling with boxes on the other side. I spun down the hall. Past her empty study with the overhead light shining on the bare wood floor, past my study with the desk light pooling on my typewriter. I went into the living room and threw myself on our bed. It was my bed now. With the sweet musky smell of her breath on my pillow, when I hugged it.

Body oil! he tells me. Bubble bath! A happy, un-neurotic, undemanding woman who actually likes sex! He's waving his hands, hissing low; we're hunched over pies and a bottle of vino rosso at a local trattoria. Try as he might, he's incapable of accounting for her existence. Freud would have panicked. Squeezed him dry. More wine? Prego. Not that I need any urgings towards debauchery after *my* week.

Kenna, Kenna, Kenna. A Red Cross nurse in the city John Calvin built. He met her at McGill—this nice Irish Catholic girl from Babylon, Long Island who played field hockey and happened to be sitting next to him in a lecture on Greek Tragedy taught by the most famous Canadian classics scholar who was at least a decade into his dotage and utterly incomprehensible. She was lost, Paul was lost;

one of them leaned over and whispered something, both of them got hysterical, she ended up scribbling her number on his notebook as the bell rang. Ponytail, down vest. Within three weeks they'd discovered half a dozen thoroughly obscene uses for strawberry jam, none involving toast. Who knew what she'd seen in him? He had more hair at that point, maybe she thought he looked like Sophocles. She'd grown up around Jews.

Anyway, they kept in touch—she left for nursing school end of sophomore year, he finished up, went to law school, met the famous Liz, got his heart broken by the fiendish Judith. Why did I ever get the idea he was a monk? Augustine wallowing in Carthaginian squalor is more like it. Any fantasies of celibacy he might once have entertained were strictly a function of exhaustion.

Geneva was marvelous. Like old friends who just happen to have a dirty little secret. She worked during the day, he played tourist—stuffing himself on Swiss chocolates, staring at absurdly overpriced watches in store windows, making a pilgrimage to Calvin's church. Ah, Calvin. Four hundred and fifty years ago the man returns from exile and hijacks the town—closes down the bars, prohibits dancing, makes adultery punishable by death, preaches fifty sermons a week about the depravity of human nature, invites rebel Catholics from all over Europe to come and join the fun, which makes the Pope go Aha! Den of Iniquity! because why else would so many monks and nuns be turning in their hair shirts and fleeing north? Then he marries an Anabaptist—with trepidation; we all know how perilous the marriage bed is—and when she dies eight years later the nicest thing he can say is, She never interfered with my work. What a guy! His chair in Saint-Pierre Cathedral looks like something you might strap a serial murderer into.

Marvelous Geneva with its clean people and clean streets gets boring fast. Kenna takes him out clubbing one night to hear a Swiss lounge group called Feline. The lead singer obviously has Tina Turner in mind—fishnet stockings, legs from here to there, lips curled in sexual agony—but there's something bizarre about a black girl with a voice like Catherine Deneuve crooning "What's Love Got to Do With It" to a roomful of tipsy Alpenhorn salesmen. Not to mention the drummer. How is it possible for one human being to murder that much swing with every touch of a stick? Unless, of course, you were born and raised in a land that prides itself on precision chronometers. Rolexes do not get down. So much for Calvin's legacy.

Last day he's in town Kenna takes the afternoon off and they head into the mountains. He figures he'll sit back and leave the driving to her; nobody warns him about the roads. You think you've seen narrow? Twisting? Sheer? Honking your horn around every blind corner, praying the other guy isn't yodeling along with his car radio. Halfway up they pull off, park, get out. Mont Blanc is in your face— two or three miles away but you'd swear you could touch it, across a chasm so deep he's afraid to look down. Air so fresh you could bottle the stuff. Nobody says a word. A plane buzzes by; it might as well be a gnat. Kenna crouches and plucks something. He closes his eyes and lets her feed him. What does he know from wild blackberries? He's ready to pitch a tent and stay.

Next morning they're at the station, she's putting him on a train for Bologna. He's happy, she's happy; one more night and he'd have been a basket case. There *is* no moral of the story. Next year in Babylon. Of course the moment he gets on and stares at her cute face through the window he feels like shit. How often in this life do we encounter someone with whom we can share the deepest, most gloriously raunchy part of our souls? People tend to sell true lust short.

Bologna is marginally less boring than Geneva, chiefly due to the threat of death hanging over he who ventures forth to do battle with teeming hordes of Vespas, Lambrettas, Piaggios and Fiats. Six-way intersections, nothing resembling a stoplight. He visits a few museums—the great art's all down in Florence, it's hard to get worked up about a town where the main cathedral looks like an aborted Lego project because the reigning priests back in 1390 diverted funds to build themselves a palace. Oh for Dante's world! He spends his afternoon on the steps of the thing, nose buried in *The Inferno*, trying to figure out which Circle of Hell they should be consigned to. Carnal sins are only the Second, so he's in fairly good shape. At night he descends into the Third and engages in unrepentant Gluttony. Tortellini! Tagliatelli! Virgin olive oil slathered on everything! He speaks no Italian; waving his hands accomplishes miracles. Waiters, maitre d's. The only one not convinced is his landlady; thirty-five thousand a night she has the nerve to charge for a tiny cubicle with no shower! Then he finds the government-regulated prices on the back of his door. Dante knew whereof he spoke—Fraud!—when he dreamed up the Eighth Circle. Into which of ten concentric chasms shall we cast her? The Second, where Flatterers are immersed in filth? The Seventh, where Thieves are tormented by serpents? He crawls out of bed after two nights, packs, leaves the money the Emilia-Romagna Chamber of Commerce claims he owes her on the bed, and sneaks down the back steps.

Of course his conscience begins to flay him alive. Would he have done the same thing in London? Not to mention the possibility of practical consequences. An eye for an eye sounds terrific in theory; bread and water in a Sicilian dungeon do not. He takes a room at Pensione Marconi—pricey, clean, shower included—and hides out for a day, lost in the Ninth Circle. Violence to kin, traitor to country. Two sinners frozen in one hole, gnawing on each other's heads. Where does Dante come up with such madness? Dinner that night—chicken cacciatore—is tasteless; he keeps expecting Vito & Sons to burst through the front door with sawed-off shotguns. Don't ask how he sleeps. In the morning he's up early. A couple of old men on bicycles, pigeons huddled in front of the unfinished cathedral. Why should his heart be pounding like this? Approaching the place makes him feel nauseous. Ten thousand in an envelope shoved through a slot in the front door. An hour later the cafes are open, motor scooters are spiraling out of nowhere, he's sitting on a sunny terrace with a cappuccino and an apricot danish—so light and sweet it barely exists. Italians! And his book. Dante and Virgil have just climbed back out of the muck. "Thence issuing, we beheld again the stars." Good stuff, if you're in the mood.

I shave in the morning while Paul pores over train schedules—we're heading down to Florence after breakfast—but it makes no difference: the bird of bone-deep exhaustion is squatting on my soul. The faintest trace of soreness is hovering in my throat, threatening to engorge. All forward momentum has been lost. I dig listlessly through my pack, hunting for the long-ignored bottle of Vitamin C. Sudden pockets of rancidity kick up through pervasive running-shoe stench. Something has died down there. Hacked to pieces, shoved in a picnic cooler, left to putrefy.

Breakfast is a glass of lukewarm cappuccino at a stand-up bar next to the pensione, a small leafy pastry glazed with sugar sand. Warm breezes brush my arms, make me shiver. The world is glittery, brittle. My Panama hat resting on my Mouse seems like a relic from a distant Golden Age. I ask the bartender for a jus d'orange; he raises his eyebrows, mutters something musical I can't understand. Paul clears his throat, sticks up a finger. Un arancia, per favore. The guy digs a small bottle out of his cooler and pops the cap. The stuff is sweetened, processed, barely enough to wash down four C's.

The Bologna train station is morning-cool, a bustling oasis. Paul rolls his eyes; maybe the Red Army Faction will refrain from blowing us up? We heave off our packs, affix ourselves to the tail of a biglietti ordinari line. A stooped older woman with her head wrapped in a red bandanna pulls in behind. We inch forward to give her space; she inches forward, refusing to waste it. Her tracheal rasp digs into the small of my back. She cranes her neck, straining to see the ticket window. Minutes go by. We are fifth from the front; she has eased around my left and pulled even. Paul and I stare. She refuses to acknowledge our existence. The line inches forward; she moves eight to our six. Fourth from the front, third. The ticket window next to ours suddenly closes, standing an entire line on Paul's right flank. An infuriated man is waving his hands and shouting through the slot where the CHIUSO sign has just been put up. The decamping clerk shrugs and disappears. His line wavers, eyes us, then sags left in a grumbling, melting wave which quickly turns into a free-for-all rush towards our window. Everybody has something to say about this; our little old lady turns out to be the loudest hand-waver of the bunch. Evil eyes, dead cattle, boys committing unspeakable acts on mothers. So much for the Roman Empire.

The train south is a swooping downward glide through cool musty tunnels, interspersed with flashes of summer, fragrant and yearning. The movement does me good. I sit in a window seat facing Paul—he's lost in the *Purgatorio*—with my journal open, nibbling on my pen, thinking about Helen and Lonnie. Images of their love-making crowd around and beat at me like a cave of panicked bats. I sigh, fighting the pressure in my chest. Suddenly I'm coughing. Paul glances up. Would it interest me to know that the Black Death ravaged more than a third of the Florentine population in 1348? My ears pop, adjusting to the new altitude. We've fallen a long way in the past hour.

The train station in Florence is a feeding-frenzy of young Americans paging frantically through slabby orange copies of *Let's Go*, triangulating cheap hotels, darting off to attack. Paul and I quickly decide on Pensione La Tua Casa—"your home-away-from-home"—on the Piazza Santa Maria Novella. A young woman trots by; she has an extravagantly wide jaw, thick black hair with sunglasses pushed back, a belted white t-shirt worn tunic-style reading BORN IN THE US WRANGLER TAKE THE LEAD AMERICAN OVERSEAS. She tosses her mane in a way that suggests frozen ices brought by runners, a palace in the hills. This town could be a revelation. We heave on packs and flow towards the glimmering portal, a beckoning summer noon. The streets are a blur of young women in tight jeans careening blithely by on motorbikes: Piaggio, Garelli, Vespa, Malaquiti, Aprilia, Garosa, Gabbiano. We veer up a side street; sudden whiffs of damp plaster curl out of cool dark basement workshops.

The pensione is two flights up a gloomy staircase. A little girl hugging a huge tomcat is perched on the top step; she scoots aside, turns and stares. The short greying guy at the front desk is named Frank. He tells us to cut the shit and speak American after Paul stutters through our basic pitch. The young woman at his side murmurs something in Italian and peels a couple of bath towels off a stack next to the parrot cage. The bird shrieks. Frank in his blue blazer is seventy-seven and from Chicago, originally. Tobacco-stained fingers, thick greyish eyebrows that join above his nose. He lights up as we stand there, flattered by our amazement. American? Christ, he used to push a cab out in Chi back in forty-six, after the war. Northside. Southside was where the niggers lived. It may be different these days, he don't know. Out in Vegas before that. Thirty-three, thirty-four—when Vegas was still an Indian town. Government gave 'em reservations. You win a hundred-dollar bill back then, a hundred bucks was a big thing. Like a thousand now. More than that. He pauses, ash teetering on the end of his butt. Eases himself into a chair next to the parrot cage. As he was saying: Chi during prohibition, when Capone was around. Hey, Sinatra just played a show up in Milano last year, they paid the guy half a million and he's only three years younger than guess who.

Frank's head is tilted back; he's humming an aria. The woman behind the desk suddenly explodes in a burst of Italian. The girl on the top step drops her cat with a thump and flees. Frank comes to, curses the woman back with equal fluency, creaks to his feet and finishes copying down our passport numbers. She hands us towels and makes no attempt to smile.

The room is clean and cheerful, with two beds that sag moderately when we drop our packs. And a view: pigeons speckling quadrants of mowed lawn in the piazza below, huddling under the green-and-white-striped arches of Santa Maria Novella. Which happens to be the church, Paul informs me, where Boccaccio's Dirty Dozen holed up during the Black Death and told each other the series of delightfully filthy tales known as *The Decameron*. Parrot shrieking down the hall behind us. I swallow, wincing at the lump in my throat.

[W]e used to go and stand on the bridges and admire the Arno. It is popular to admire the Arno. It is a great historical creek with four feet in the channel and some scows floating around. It would be a very plausible river if they would pump some water into it. They all call it a river, and they honestly think it is a river, do these dark and bloody Florentines. They even help out the delusion by building bridges over it. I do not see why they are too good to wade.

—Mark Twain
The Innocents Abroad

It's the only one the Nazis didn't blow up during the war, Paul tells me.

We're leaning over the side, spooning gelato—limone and cioccolato for me, fragola and stratciatella for him—and watching a couple of Italian guys feed the fish. A lot of them down there like tiny brown maggots, rippling and churning just below the surface. Every time a morsel of bread drops, a few leap through, jaws snapping. A couple of monsters lurking around the piles, eighteen inches long and thick as a child's thigh. The Italian guys whistle as they toss in the remaining half loaf. An explosion of gnashing, thrashing, sudden muscular wrenchings as the big guys fight it out. Then a tan scull slices through—prow blossoming out of nowhere, pair of college girls with pony tails and singlets, bare shoulders heaving, paddles dipping and rising—and the fish scatter, gone.

The stuff is melting before I can spoon it, pale yellow and dark brown swirling together, a flavor with no name.

Much good sunglass want me buy you, says a voice on my shoulder. Cheap price. Sexy.

He's leopard black and wearing Wayfarers, a flowered shirt, jeans, sandals. Attaché case held open. Vuarnets, Carreras, Rolexes. Fingers lovingly stroking each item.

No thank you, says Paul.

American? he exclaims, flashing a smile of practiced astonishment. He hooks out a pair with lizardy dark lenses, holds them towards us. Risky Business, he urges. Bang bang. Sexy.

Canadian, Paul mutters. Boring.

When he finds out we're from New York he pulls out a small address book, jabs his finger at an African name. 2331 Melrose Aves, Bronx New York. Good friend this one, he says. Soon him go visit. Buy everybody Fifth Avenue sunglass. Trump is best place. Wet sun make better for umbrella. He glances at us hopefully, heaves a daypack down off his shoulder. Umbrella?

Next time, Paul says.

He shrugs, closes his attaché case, swings away.

We stroll across to the upriver side, past a guy demonstrating his remarkable dancing sprite for a small crowd. Cardboard body parts, black thread for limbs. He waves his hand from a distance and it jumps, shimmies, collapses, leaps up. Obviously a scam but impossible to figure out. I chuck my empty cup in a trashcan.

I wonder if Africans ever take vacations the way we do, I say.

Paul slurps a spoonful of cream-colored gelato. I've always assumed they just stay at home and try to avoid getting mauled by lions.

An overweight young woman in tan hiking shorts is sitting on the balustrade to our left, leg propped up, sketching. Thigh dimpled with cellulite. She glances up, back at her pad.

Vacations are basically a Western invention, I say. Slave in an office fifty weeks a year and get two weeks off in which you're supposed to live.

He tosses his cup after mine. Come to Jamaica.

It's like, Get as far away as possible, drink Pina Coladas, fuck anything that moves, and regain your humanity around happy natives.

I glance at the young woman. She's trying hard to ignore us.

Paul removes his glasses and begins to clean. I suppose you could call the annual pilgrimage to Mecca a sort of vacation.

Yeah, but that's the Middle East.

North African Muslims.

Right.

Except for the fact that women are strictly prohibited and you're forced to walk barefoot through the desert for six months without a bath singing the praises of Allah in the company of spiteful camels.

You're such a racist, I laugh.

He spreads his hands. Who said anything about race? The Jews are just as bizarre. Since when does God go around delivering World-Historical lectures from the depths of a burning bush?

The young woman looks up from her pad. What about the Australian aborigines? she says. They go on walkabouts.

Her name is Cynthia. A senior at Boston University—marketing/anthro—and eyes that twinkle in a vaguely unnerving way. She's sketching the Arno's north bank, where half a dozen young women are shouldering inverted sculls on a sliver of worn lawn. Romanesque arcades shading the river road. Her line is billowy but you can tell what things are. She thinks we're a couple of very interesting guys.

Paul waves her away. You wouldn't recognize us back in New York.

We're boring, I agree. We sit around libraries all day reading books.

She dimples her cheeks. You don't look like the boring type, either one of you.

We're not the worst, Paul sighs. Most of our classmates are incurable sociopaths who spend all day hypnotizing themselves into believing absolutely ridiculous theories about literature.

Not to mention moral sleazebags, I add.

McKay is...how shall I put this? He clasps a hand to his chest. Recovering from a broken heart.

I jump up and balance on a grey plastic sewer pipe. That's one way of putting it.

Oh ho, Cynthia chuckles ruefully. I could tell you a few stories.

Would we be interested in buying a bottle of wine? She knows a store just off the end of the bridge. Paul and I exchange looks.

Ten minutes later we're sitting on the curb of the bridge roadway getting delightfully trashed. Two plastic cupfuls of vino bianco on a gelato-primed gut; musty-castle smell of damp brick when I lean back against a column. Cynthia's bare thighs look huge and puffy between ours. June midafternoon in Firenze.

Will somebody please tell me why Italian women all wear those skimpy dresses? I ask plaintively as a couple of live ones wriggle by.

Butt-huggers, Cynthia murmurs.

Pheromones, Paul cackles, saluting with his cup. Amore.

He's drunk, I whisper in Cynthia's ear. Shut him up.

She gives me big eyes. You think so, huh?

I grab the bottle and refill his lifted cup. By any means necessary.

McKay thinks you're drunk, she says, bumping his shoulder. Wine sloshes out.

In the immortal words of Albert Collins... he says, holding up his finger.

Bootsy Collins, I add, dodging Cynthia's shoulder.

Shake your booo-ty, she sings.

...I ain't drunk, I'm just drinkin'.

She leans back on her hands, shakes brown curls out of her face. So tell me about Dante.

A sudden thunderstorm has come up and we're scrambling, retreating to a covered archway on the bridge, wrapping ourselves in the beach towel I've stowed in my daypack. The skies open; lightning crackles across the river, drops spattering the surface into washed-out green. Lukewarm mist fans our faces. Cynthia smells fresh and lemony, despite her bulk; Paul smells like Paul. Wine bottle in the middle, warmed by many hands.

Well guys, she chirps.

I wake in the morning with plugged sinuses, an octave-doubled cough, low-res soul. The bird of bone-deep exhaustion has become a nesting grackle. Paul putters around our room—tufts of mossy brown hair sprouting from pale shoulders, friar's paunch—while I savor the calculus of pain generated by attempts at swallowing my own saliva. His hand is moist on my forehead. No, I do not have a fever. Yes, my attendance on today's field trip is required. No, that second cup of gelato after last night's fettucini alfredo was not an inspired idea. Yes, the wines of Tuscany may well contain congestion-inducing histamines. No, he doesn't have much sympathy for me. Yes, she most certainly is. San Gimignano, a medieval hill town. Dante country.

Frank is smoking, coughing, making entries in a ledger as we drop off our keys at the front desk. Same blue blazer sifted with dandruff and ash. Let him know tonight about tomorrow night. Wraaaaack! squawks the parrot. My eyes are bleared and oily as I spoon crystals through foam at the cafe downstairs. Paul munches fastidiously on a glazed flaky elephant ear, dipping his head as crumbs scatter. Gulp and go. We're dodging across intersections, freezing at beeped horns, no part of this dance. Cynthia waiting at the bus station is plump rosy cheeks and knock-kneed thighs cinched into hiking shorts and safari shirt with a knotted red bandanna around her throat. She hands us tickets and we heave ourselves on.

What would she like to know about the divine comedian? I'm leaning back and swooning, lost in Paul's professorial murmur as we loop up out of town. We tend to put great poets on a pedestal instead of seeing them for the petty, vengeful, woefully unbalanced—albeit talented—crazies they were. Not to mention the troubadours. Forget about Bob Dylan; back then every coffeehouse wastrel wanted to be Rainbaut de Vaqueiras. Get yourself a lute, a couple of willing joglars—your basic twelfth-century roadie equivalent—and a sheaf of juicy love songs addressed to a well-born married lady who you may not actually have dallied with but have in any case conceived an agonized and hopelessly unrequitable passion for. "I love with a love so perfect that I often weep, finding in my grief a kind of ecstasy," etcetera. Hot stuff, especially in the Provencal tongue which even your lowliest court lackey could understand. Arnaut Daniel, Bertran de Born, Raimon de Miraval. Oh for the days when giants walked the earth!

We change busses in Poggibonsi—Cynthia gives off sweet lemony fumes when she brushes past me—and wind upward into patchworked green hills. The Tuscan countryside, Paul sighs, savoring the words like fine wine. I slide open my window and shove my snout through, straining for summer against blocked sinuses. The town appears, teetering grey towers clustered on a walled wooded hilltop. Paul cocks a cynic's eye: You think Donald Trump cares from art when he builds a skyscraper? You're a medieval nobleman bored stiff because the Renaissance isn't due for another hundred and fifty years, so you pay five hundred serfs a penny apiece to put up a tower three feet taller than your cousin's down the block. Seven hundred years later the Nazis come along with bombs and miss. Welcome to civilization.

The bus disgorges us on the edge of a dusty square just outside the wall. Hot breezes ruffle our hair. We walk through the stone gate—LUISA TI AMO! EMILIANO—spray-painted overhead—and into the shaded cool of a narrow inclined street. Wind chimes tinkle; alleys veer off, dead-end in shiny cars. We buy a large brown loaf of pane fresco, hunk of Bel Paese and three cantaloupes in one shop, two pale green bottles of Vernaccia di San Gimignano in another. Cynthia's Italian is halting but awesomely functional. A pair of stuffed wild boars stand tusky, snuffling guard in a charcuterie doorway; we emerge with sliced prosciutto, butcher-papered and fragrant. Time shudders as we work our way uphill. The street opens out into a sun-washed plaza; old men in short-sleeved shirts lean back in shaded chairs next to stone walls, watching everything. Hunger drives us upward, past the church brooding in massive calm. Brick walkways loop through overhanging arches, veer up flights of steps, become packed gravel paths lined with high hedges teeming with iridescent emerald beetles mating and feeding. Hot lizards scamper and freeze in the dust.

The town garden, when we come to it, seems to have been plucked from the pages of some obscure medieval legend, set down here at the top of the world for our private benefit. Lots of unmowed grass, spaced overgrown olive trees, three or four vaulting firs clustered around a well, crabbed fruit trees hugging the surrounding wall. A cock crows from a fenced hutch in the far corner; a prowling brown tabby spies us, stares, bolts. A Nordic couple strolls past us and out through the arched entryway. The grass is fragrant, beckoning, voluptuous. We throw down our burdens and fall, sighing. I pull out my Swiss Army knife. The wine is strong and slightly fizzy; the melon is trembling locked-up nectar leaping into our mouths, dribbling seeds, heavenly.

Mmmm, she purrs afterward. Stroking our hair; her body our pillow, guts burbling against the back of my head. We're bathed in warm oily light, floating in a charmed clearing. Paul's voice droning somewhere over the crest of her hips. Who can read Castiglione's *Book of the Courtier* today and not be astonished? Five hundred years before deconstruction and the man is self-conscious to the point of meltdown about his discourse. Tuscan usage this, corrupted Lombard that. Only in Italy, land of a thousand dysfunctional city-states. Our ideal courtier must be beautiful of countenance, born of a noble and genteel family—i.e., no hook-nosed Shylocks need apply. Bitter? Who's bitter? Let his young Adonises gracefully lance each other over the honor of bored duchesses; this scholarly Jew would rather live to write books.

Later we rise groaning, drag ourselves up one last flight of steps, look out over the wall at terraced farmland—Paul snaps a few pictures so we'll know we've been here—and waddle back down into town. A balding mustached guy with a harp between his legs is lounging in an arcade next to the church, plucking arpeggios for tips. Eyes flashing with quiet joy when he sings. I swoon in the shade—sinuses plugged, not understanding a word—while Paul and Cynthia get religious. A minute later they're back; no shorts allowed. We buy gelatos around the corner—Cynthia's mirtillo purples her tongue—and wander down past the stuffed wild boars, out through the front gate into dusty heat to catch our bus.

All I want to do when we get back is collapse—beehive roar of motorbikes filtering up through wooden shutters—but the room next door has been occupied by two friendly young women in flow-ered shorts who have legs and speak English. Annie is Jewish, from Melbourne, wearing thick black flip-flops with striped nylon thongs; bare shoulders like a butterfly stroker and an accent marinated in marsupial sex. Gloria is Chicana, from L.A.—small perfect mouth, thick glasses—and studies computer science at Santa Cruz. She talks Spanish at the Italians, they talk Italian at her, everybody understands. She and Annie met at The World's Most Beautiful Youth Hostel up in Verona. Annie's been on the road for six months and has another year to go. The Austrailan way, because plane stubs anywhere are so pricey.

Cynthia is surprised when we show up at her pensione at eight as planned with two extra girls. I can't keep track of who or what I want anyway, apart from sleep. We float through dusky back streets pocketed with leather shops, restaurants in open cellars where men with greased Elvis hair saw at huge candlelit steaks. Cheerless grey palazzi loom on all sides. Paul is lecturing about Medici and treachery, the necessity of fortifications. These were not nice men. Caricaturists lounge in directors' chairs along the floodlit marble flank of the Uffizzi as we round a corner, framed by big noses and toothy grins: Madonna, Woody Allen, Paul Newman, Reagan in a cowboy hat and star-spangled diapers.

We fall into chairs at a cafe fronting the Piazza della Signoria. Paul gestures at the castellated clock tower of Palazzo Vecchio, Michelangelo's David and Bandinelli's Hercules guarding the front doors like so much rippling spotlit alabaster flesh. How many her-etics were boiled in oil that we might feast our eyes on such sights? When I squint I can see David's hands, which do seem big. Hercules has a naked guy by the hair, yanked down to crotch height, ready to club. Vino rosso for everybody.

One glass and Cynthia and I are alone in a velvety charmed circle, continuing this afternoon's bus conversation. Of course women have the right to be agents of their own destiny. That wasn't Helen's problem. Saying she loved me and sleeping with other guys was her problem. Cynthia understands. She rubs my bare leg like an old friend. Maybe the woman just needs time to find herself. Maybe she's missing me right now. My problem is I worry too much. I'm too tense. Did I know that a glass of red wine a day prevents heart attacks? The French just did a study. She clinks my glass, eyes chuckling. Here's to prevention.

We're on our third round when two strolling guitarists in matching black jeans, white t-shirts and loafers approach and begin serenading us with "Blue Suede Shoes." They have wicked smiles and can't sing but pull it off on sheer heart. Cynthia and Annie bravo; Paul tosses a thousand-lire note into the beret proffered by the huskier guy with darting eyes. They bow. Skinny guy whips out two pairs of Wayfarers and slips one on, holds the second out. Lizardy cool cats with scowls and big noses: viva il Blues Brothers. Halfway through their bouncy rendition of "Sweet Home Chicago" I pull out my A-harp—flattened, rusted, reeking of last week—and take a solo. They insist with large gestures that I join them. I demur. They insist. I stagger to my feet, jostle shoulders, blow two lame choruses and try to match their moves. Paul leads the cheers; Cynthia's eyes are glowing.

Their names are Roberto and Giancarlo—Bobby and Johnny— and set-break is at our table, wine courtesy of the beret. Bobby does the talking; Johnny grins, shrugs, scratches the back of his head. Bobby he's always happy making the knowledge of American musician. Best music for all the world coming from America. Elvis Presley, Bruce Springsteen. Best girls, too. Only two boys talking for three

Jersey girls at this table? No good. Everybody gotta work too hard! He and Johnny gonna help out. Leaning forward to light the cigarette he's just offered Annie. Gloria and Johnny are suddenly chattering in two languages; Johnny is a flurrying flyweight come to life, all hands slicing air. Bobby touches his chest. He's being born in Firenze. Not like so many Roman boys with the talking only to girls. Makes a scornful face as he blows smoke. These boys, they are knowing maybe four words in American. How are you, you like Roma, how long you stay, you like Italian boys? No good. He's talking with all people, also boys, asking them, Tell me something from your country, is it nice place there? Then maybe next time he gonna fly in a plane and stay with them cheap!

Wine flows. Johnny's pulling out a crumpled sheet of paper and insisting I proofread a love song he's written in English. He writes the way he talks, with his hand on his heart. Always he's wanting to go from America, do I know this? Possible he's born in a wrong country. Hey, he's gonna show me a picture—beautiful American girl from when he's singing the song. Reaching into his hip pocket, pulling out a purse. Other Italian boys? Pfft. Make love with this one, that one, all different one. Not him. He was very fortune one time. Summer passed—he's only boy singing by Uffizzi step, Johnny doesn't come. Then this girl from Flemington, New Jersey. He's gonna cry she's so sweet. Look.

The party breaks up soon after that. Bobby and Johnny have to work, we're beat. I hear myself volunteer to walk Cynthia home, which meets with general approval—Paul has keyed on Annie—and leaves the two of us tripping down a back street giggling hysterically, pursued by a balding heavyset German in a grey suit and monocle who seems to have fallen in love with Cynthia as she got up from the table. He could be a university professor and is as drunk as we are. We yell German-sounding nonsense syllables in response and he finally falls back, muttering.

She pulls me into the shade when we reach her pensione. Her mouth is larger than Helen's. I have to come up for air—sinuses completely blocked—but at least I'm not dripping. Her bare thighs look puffy and formless in the dim light. I brush my fingers across one and she shudders, chuckling naughtily.

She asks me if I'd like a massage as I follow her upstairs. I flop across her bed, groaning. Her hands are expert—double-jointed thumbs, she chirps—and my shoulders crunch with delicious pain. Her breath rustles in my ear, thighs pinioning my back. When she rolls me over I have nothing left except the bulge in my shorts, which can't complain. She's gentle. She seems to like me. She knows what to do.

An old woman is feeding a flock of pigeons when I stick my head out our window next morning. She and they own the piazza, except for the guy dozing on the grass. His hair is in better shape than mine. Paul is brushing his teeth. He can't believe me. Two weeks I've been trying to get laid—sparing no expense of spirit, he might add—and now the gods see fit to bless me and I'm complaining?

Not exactly. I'm standing by the window with a flutter in the pit of my stomach. The brick sidewalk four stories down is calling. Suicidal is the wrong word. What bothers me are the invisible energy beams curling up and over the windowsill. The pull from down there. Images of skulls cracking like broken eggs. Italy is not supposed to produce such images in otherwise normal yolks. I step back, rub my bare arms—cold's about the same—and flop into bed. Big favor is requested of dear friend. Surrogate courtiership to fair maiden, with attendant perks if offered. The Uffizi at noon. Regrets. I need to collect my wits or I will die.

Paul is confused but willing. He's noticed I seem a little moody lately. Would I care to join him for a prima colazione in the dining room downstairs? I would not? This is the clearest sign yet of mental derangement. He will console said maiden and leave me to my own devices. Ciao.

I wait a moment after he's shut the door, then glide across the room, heave outer shutters and inner windows closed, shove bolts home, grab my pack, and upend it over my unmade bed. T-shirts, socks, bits of paper, leaves, sand. I reach into the maw and yank fresh sediment loose at each pause in the flow. The smells are diverse and overwhelming, tending towards the marine; life poised to drag itself dripping out of primeval muck. Last layer to come unstuck is my Eastern Mountain Sports poncho, used precisely once: that first rainy day in Paris, two-and-a-half weeks ago. That was another life. That life has somehow turned into this life. I dig frantically through the pile. Everything is jumbled: scattered francs and centimes from my time with Finney and Bill; green cotton sweater smeared with tequila-vomit; Eurrail schedule with cover torn off; greasy paper bag filled with Brie-mush and soggy bread crusts from Dr. Livingstone's party; Joey's address on Long Island; Nicole's in Tannersville; Bill's SALVATION: DON'T LEAVE HOME WITHOUT IT t-shirt, reeking of coconut oil and sweat. I snatch up the blue nylon stuff bag, pop the tie-cord release and shake it empty, pull back gagging. Was *that* where I put the wild apricots? My running clothes stink of death.

Both journals—old and new—are in my hands as I fall onto Paul's bed. The old one is stained with strawberry jam, various greases and tannins; looped wire spine has been yanked loose at one end. The new one, miraculously, is pristine. Smells vaguely of rotten fruit but sun-bleaching will cure that. I heave myself off the bed, then remember the invisible energy beams and fall back. I toss it aside and grab my filled-up baby. Paging forward through so much captured life—different inks, scrawls, moods—makes me dizzy. That first shitfaced entry in Avignon, the night I met Joey and Michel, is barely legible. Bill's stories!

I flip to the bottom of the last entry and scratch today's date and time. Longest day of the year. If you can put down everything you've done since Tuesday morning you will be okay. The story will come clear. A moral will emerge. Direction for future action.

I scribble until my hand cramps—a shower has just come up on the Ponte Vecchio—then heave myself at the sink, scourge with cold water and pitch back in. Some things I can't bring myself to write down. A waste of shame. Discretion is the better part of style.

Only three blank pages left when I finish and I'm rereading, editing for flow, then slamming shut and leaping up. Gotcha! Bidet cranked on, rummaging in a zippered pack-pocket for soap powder. Suds apocalypse. Falling to my knees, breathing through my mouth, scrubbing stains out of underpants. The pair I wore from Nice to Bologna are a sight. My cutoffs threaten to walk away, then drown and soften. Rinsing in the sink until cold waters run clear, wringing dry, throwing open windows, shutters, everything. Sun streams in. The old woman is gone; pigeons have scattered. I hang my wash, humming.

Running away from town along the river road—fifteen minutes out, Ponte Vecchio a smudge over my shoulder—and the body is a miracle this noon. Quads of steel, Mercury-winglets on both ankles. Call me Piaggio. Sputtering motorino herds pass, fan out across two lanes, then brake where the bridges cross as I glide up and over, dodging side-beeps, sacrificing myself to the god of flow. His clean machine smells of Ivory Snow. Sinuses thawing like slush on Vermont backcountry roads, melting and dripping. The heart should hurt, hard as I'm working, but doesn't. Opening up instead of clenching: petal by petal, blown wide. Pouring myself into the world. This is heaven.

Veering onto a dirt path under overhanging trees as the road ends, adjusting my stride and skimming on. The Arno shimmering down below, cool green satin hemmed by walls, a brambly scramble if I stumble left. Butterflies leap up. You were born to die. Barest extra push of the ball of each foot and my stride lengthens, you can feel the governor swing open as the power plant bears down, tension rippling through humming belts. Grace under pressure; fire in your chest. Ease off and the flames weaken, falling away from the stake.

Leaning like a biker as I arc through a gap in the trees, everything suddenly cools, I'm gliding through woods along ribbon-smooth macadam. Birdcalls overhead drowned out by my rasp and slap. Whistles over my shoulder, a vague whirring quickly swelling as I turn and freeze: a thirty-bike racing pack swoops down, parts like holy seas, washes over me, vanishes around a corner up ahead. Then two small boys on big wobbling ten speeds trying to catch up. I break into a jog and lope after them. The woods smell like hidden flowers, cool-rooted.

Swinging around the corner and holding my line, floating out of the woods into a grassy rutted field. Upturned white bonnets of Queen Anne's Lace; I'm dipping, plucking a handful, squeezing tiny flowerlets for the wild carrot smell. Down-fluffed dandelions, scallion-clumped wild garlic. Six guys playing soccer at the far end. Crickets rustling as I lope through shaggy grass, hugging the perimeter, slowed suddenly by their sound, stopping. Panting. The ones closest to me have stopped singing. I take a step forward. Silence fans out. I stand motionless, quieting my breath. Yells in the distance; somebody's just scored. I glance up. An elderly couple in angled garden chairs is lounging on the sidelines not far from me, shaded by overhanging oaks. The man murmurs something musical and disgusted, gesturing at unseen phantoms; the woman shakes her head, clucks, smoothes her dress. Two young guys with motorcycle helmets just past them, lazing in the tall grass.

Lying on my back with hands cradling my head, pillowed in soft green blades, cooled by the old folks' oak. Earth bearing me up. Encircled by a constellation of crickets—clicking, hesitating, then thrumming. If you knew the species you could count chirps and tell the temperature. Poisons leaching from your bones, melting through flesh, draining. Who do you love more than you love me? Chasing butterflies, inhaling summer. Lord I was born a ramblin' man. Lay me now I down to deep. And if my sky-high soul to keep.

Waking with a start as a motorcycle roars to life. The elderly couple is gone. Stretching my limbs; a long rippling shiver like a yawning cat. Two ants on my shoulder tumbling over themselves to scramble off. Flesh patterned like a pale rhino's, hatched by flattened grass.

I watch the bikers buckle helmets and zoom off, then rise. Afternoon heat swirling voluptuously against my face. Gliding into a slow jog around the field's far end, back the way I came. The cool woods suck me in. Easing off into a walk. Birds coo and ratchet in high trees. You'd never know this was Florence. Maybe Florentines feel the same way about Central Park.

Loping out of the woods further down than I entered, skin flayed by stiff shrubs. River unrolled under the sun like limpid green silk, left to right. I jog over to the concrete levee edge, crouch next to a couple of boys. Seven or eight old men are bathing in the shallows below, where water breaks over rocks. Scooping up crystal syrup. The air reaching us has been beaten into morning freshness and could heal anything. I breathe and stare. Flesh hanging loosely from arm bones, skimpy suits cradling bulges. My eyes are suddenly wet. Stripping off my running shoes and socklets, picking my way down the steps like somebody's young bride. Tiny pebbles prick my bones. The cool waters shiver through me when I touch. A couple of men look up, nod; one smiles and murmurs something I can't understand. He's missing an arm. I wade out half blind into the deeper part, mud squinching between my toes. Then I'm in, I'm in, I am in.

My sneeze wakes Paul in the morning. I'm standing next to my bed, head wet from the shower he didn't hear me slip out and take. The towel around my waist falls off just as he opens his eyes. I catch it and rewrap.

You didn't see that, I say.

His gaze is humorless. I must be having a nightmare.

Well I feeeeel so baaaaaad, I hum, slapping hair out of my eyes as I pivot towards the dresser mirror. The face has looked worse. I yank a tissue out of the box and clear my sinuses, a hawking snotty blow.

Would you prefer to be cremated or devoured by rodents? he asks mildly.

So how'd your lunch date go? I ask, snatching a clean pair of underpants out of my pack and yanking them up.

You're in trouble.

She was upset?

Wouldn't you have been?

Shit.

Which is not to say inconsolable.

I rake my hair back. You did tell her about noon today?

She'll be waiting for you.

I toss the towel, yank on clean cutoffs, button up as I pad towards the window. The morning air is silky and cool. Green candy cane church off to the right, slashed with light.

It's gonna be another hot one, I murmur.

He grunts.

I twist and inspect my shoulders. The burn has faded to peeling skin, like a snake shedding.

I still can't figure out why I slept with her.

Weakness of the flesh.

I mean it's not like I was wildly attracted.

You enjoyed yourself, I gather.

She must hate my guts.

I wouldn't say hate.

She's confused.

Confused is a good word.

Maaaan, I sigh.

I'm assuming your day off went well since you were dead to the world when I came in.

I'll live. I leap onto my bed, bounce, flip onto my back.

Our pensione's stone stairwell has remarkable acoustics, I discover while trudging up the two flights after cappuccino and brioches next door. You'd need a pre-CBS Fender reverb unit to come close. The concierge's daughter stares as I approach her top-step perch, hugged cat wriggling in terror. I uncork a wahed yelp, then hold out my harp like a magician giving away his best trick. Chromium glint against streaking grey fur. She hesitates, twists her arms bashfully like twin corkscrews, reaches out, touches, pulls away as though burnt. Giggles.

Frank is whistling behind the desk. Christ, you'd think you were back in Chi hearing music like that. He lights up and sucks a smoky mouthful, hand masking his mustache. Ever hear of the Maxwell Street Market? They called it Jewtown back then—the niggers did, the wops, everybody insulting everybody, no hard feelings. He exhales, works his shoulders. Pushing a cab down Wabash Sunday morning, only place you could get coffee was the colored lady's diner. Nate's Deli. Hell if he knows. Some old-timer sells out, you keep the name. Vacant lot next door, that's where the hoedown was—guitars, harmonicas, hubcaps, you name it. He's never seen a colored who couldn't bang on something and make music. Hey, good luck to you. He's whistling "Sweet Georgia Brown" as he hands me my key.

An hour later I'm back on the street, struggling to stay saved amid the swirl of Florentine traffic. The flesh is willing but the spirit is mercurial. Moral fogs waft through half-opened windows; salvation is an unstable amalgam of fragrant turf, inhaled breezes, blinding sun, and luscious rivers. The rareness of sweet June days.

Cynthia is waiting for me on the Uffizi steps. Broad-faced, heavy-limbed, freckled, clean-smelling, not unpretty. She goes for the mouth as I swerve cheekward, hurt eyes crinkled into a game smile. She missed me yesterday. I'm really sorry about that, I mumble, rubbing lipstick off my jaw. At lunch—clean white tablecloth, cool fizzy mouthfuls of vino bianco—I tell her about heading north tomorrow and her face falls. She was sure I'd said Sunday, not Saturday. Her eyes close tragically. I take the nearest available hand, which allows itself to be taken. Trying to push some residue of yesterday's gleam through my fingertips. Friends? she murmurs after I invoke the word, squeezing back, doubtful. I repeat the word and hope I mean it.

After espresso and a shared tiramisu we stroll through shaded stone galleries towards the Uffizi. Caricaturists are lined up in director's chairs, waiting for likely marks. Potato noses and donkey teeth fill angled easels. We pause at the Madonna specialist and gaze at various incarnations: Material Girl, Like a Virgin, Desperately Seeking Susan. Begin with the mole and Monroe-simper, add tits and flash. I grab Cynthia and heave her towards the posing-chair; her screams draw a smile from the artist, who reaches into his duffle bag and holds up a pair of toy handcuffs. We need? We're waving him away, giggling as I let go; she's bumping me with her hip. I take her hand and we trot across the courtyard.

The Uffizi is cool, crowded, drowsy and murmurous. Kids sliding on the smooth stone floors connecting centuries. We start in Trecento with Madonnas by Giotto and Cimabue. Less black leather on these than the ones outside, fewer chains; the adoring gaze between mom and kid is what holds your attention, not a red lace bustier from Fredrick's. In Quatrocento we stumble into Paul, collapsed blissfully on a bench in front of Botticelli's *Primavera*. Did anybody say masterpiece? Not to mention the six-to-one maiden-to-swain ratio. He could talk all afternoon, and threatens to. Did we know that Mercury—young stud in the red bath towel—was modeled on Lorenzo the Magnificent, possessor of a monstrous underbite that made small children run shrieking in terror? Flattery will get you everywhere, especially if the frog prince is paying for your paint. Of course patronage cuts both ways. Give me four florins an ounce and I'll give you ultramarine made from soaked crushed lapis lazuli imported from Besarabia which will assure your blue-robed personage eternal veneration in the pantheon of saints; give me two florins an ounce and you'll be lucky to get Smucker's Grape Jelly. Your highness would prefer cheesecake? I will strip your favorite chambermaid butt naked, pose her in submissive and flagrantly erotic fashion—peekaboo hands covering the privates, etcetera—and call her Venus. Until Lorenzo croaks and Savonarola takes over, at which point bikinis are definitely a good idea.

Saturated, we stroll languidly through hallways filled with bronze heads and out into the heat of a Florentine afternoon. Tinkles of distant cafe spoons, faint rich whiff of numberless alfresco espressos. A young couple in Ray-Bans glides by; he's pedaling, she's perched sidesaddle between his arms—all thighs, hair streaming, unflappable. We've just stepped under the arcade when yells freeze us. Two boys on skateboards careen by, fly headlong off the curb in imitated Redondo Beach moves—ollieflip tailslide, alley oop kickflip—they can't quite make. Gelateria Ponte Vecchio beckons at the far end, framed like a perspective study by a dozen receding arches. I go with frutti di bosco plus annanas for Vitamin C; Paul risks croccantino plus limone. Cynthia contents herself with acqua minerale.

Up onto the bridge through a gauntlet of jeweler's shops, elbows resting on stone railings as we gaze at the river, down at fish leaping for crumbs. Cynthia murmurs wistfully; the spot where we met three days ago is behind us, next to the kiosk selling silvery commedia dell'arte masks. Paul's grimacing as he slurps straw-colored cream; now he knows sin. I'm breathing subtleties of woodland fruits mixed with pineapple.

Certain festive days demand languorous strolls along historic waterways. Paul and I escort Cynthia off the bridge and downriver with Ponte Amerigo Vespucci hovering in the distance. Yes our guide will be happy to tell of the much-maligned Florentine humanist who managed to get our country named after him. How would you feel if the king of Portugal handed you a galleon stuffed with salt mackerel and said Check Columbus' math? You're forty-three, never been to sea, an armchair cartographer in The Age of Exploration. Of course he goes. Heads due west from the Canary Islands and hopes he sees Cannibal Land before the dragons get him. Gods smile; landfall in sixty-three days. He hopscotches up the coast having strange and marvelous adventures, many involving native women, some of whom do indeed eat human flesh. Unlike Columbus, he could care less about Gold; he's here to triangulate and take notes. When provisions run low he sets sail for Lisbon, arriving home seven months after departing. He knows one thing Columbus doesn't and will die refusing to admit: India this place is not. An uncharted continent, perhaps? Three more voyages, additional calculations. In 1504 he sits down and writes his Medici patron a letter entitled *Mundus Novus*. First time that phrase has appeared in the West. He describes the wingless dragon known as the iguana and how the natives roasted and fed it to him. Delicious new fruits, delightful new flowers like the Venus flytrap. Not to mention various brown-skinned Eves. Lithe bodies, unfallen breasts. "They are not very jealous," he reports, "but they are lascivious...Out of decency I refrain from telling of the expedients they employ to satisfy their inordinate lust. They showed a great desire to have carnal knowledge of us Christians."

New World is putting it mildly. Amerigo's old one can't get enough. His letter is circulated in manuscript, copied and recopied, translated into a dozen languages. In 1507 a printer in Vicenza decides to put together a little white-men-on-the-loose anthology—Cristoforo, Amerigo, Vasco—and call it *New World and Countries Newly Discovered by Amerigo Vespucci, Florentine*, thereby erasing the distinction between the first bear to shit in the woods and the first guy to chase after him. Which makes our hero look like a swindling famegrabber instead of the modest, evenhanded—albeit lusty—scholar he was. Maps followed. Goodbye Columbia, hello America. The rest is history.

We're less than a quarter mile from Ponte Vespucci when Paul barks Follow me and veers onto steep steps carved into the brick wall separating us from the river. Up and over and suddenly we're swimming in the delicious tangled lushness of weeds, bees buzzing between tiny pink flowers. A lizard slithers across the chalky path. Paul discovered this place yesterday; grasses feather my bare thighs as we trot after him. The water-break we've seen from a distance—thin line angling across the river—turns out to be wide and flat, bleached gapped cobblestones scattered with oiled bodies. Four or five fishermen perched on the upriver side with spidery poles drooping like insect antennae.

Next time I look Paul and Cynthia are sprawled in the sun, each curled around a pad and pen. I'm belly down with my journal open, elbows on the lip; crawl three feet forward and I'm in. I yank a stalk of tall grass and chew, savoring the green corn-on-the-cob taste. Stones pressing against my ribs, water breasting away in a rippled sheet. Two young women in a scull are gliding towards me in perfect sync, paddles dripping as they ease into a turn with bare shoulders heaving, coast briefly, pull away and head upriver.

I'm flat on my back swooning when Paul calls out. Would I care to join them? Cynthia is eyeing me as she applies finishing touches to whatever she's drawing. Pen shoved in my journal—only two pages left—and I'm rolling into a crouch, drugged with sun. He's been working on a poem, which he will be happy to read. Cynthia and I bump shoulders as I flop down; he clears his throat. Firenze, he declaims, pausing to let silence accumulate:

> The streets are beautiful
> as reliquaries, and the tourists

snake through them
like a live embalming fluid

as they go to jostle
and crowd their way
into supermarkets of art
whose names roll and fall

with grand, anachronistic poetry.
Gelato, not politics,
obsesses this city now,
and ignoring the hucksters

and the human flotsam
that collects on the Ponte Vecchio,
I imagine the Arno
a huge tear of Dante's

as I watch it run towards land
so drenched with vitality
it happily bursts
into violently green hills.

Bravo! Cynthia cheers, tearing out a handful of crabgrass and sprinkling him. He shrugs: a modest pitch for immortality. She hugs her pad, too embarrassed to show. We insist, she relents. She's sketched me in recline—ankles crossed, head cradled, hayseed stalk drooping—with the river a flattened ribbon at my back, Palazzo Vecchio rising over distant rooftops like a toy castle. The face is indistinct but the runner's legs are mine. Awww, I murmur. Her cheek is moist and fragrant when I plant her reward. Paul spreads his hands. Well? Nothing worth sharing, I mumble, thumbing my pen. A few notes. Cynthia moves in for the death-tickle, I scream No! as her fingers dig in. I'll play her a song of Firenze. She lets go; I reach between my legs, pluck the toughest blade I can find, thumb-bow it. You want barbaric yawps? I am a panicked wildfowl crossed with a prolonged, triumphant female orgasm. She's clapping as I toss the flayed leaf, Paul's groaning. Dante weeps.

The tunnels are behind us. Beating upward through summer dusk—windows open, hair whipped, like ball bearings gliding along an endless race. Milano Centrale in two and a half, midnight connection to Koln.

My arms are brown as an Indian's. Back cover of this thing is smeared with mud.

Every time we stop the silence is deafening. Crickets creaking in tangled shrubs so close you could reach out and touch; smell of muskmelons breathing. Then the stationmaster's whistle and a jerk forward, we're rolling again, blurred ties shrinking to parallel lines behind the last car. Disappearing.

Chewing on my pen, which has hemorrhaged blue and will have to be chucked.

Dinner last night as a short short story: McKay And Paul Take Cynthia To Il Latini. The two young men are leaving town tomorrow; everybody is feeling festive. Why not eat at a world-famous trattoria? A friendly Italian with shirt open to the navel gives them glasses of bad vino bianco as they wait in line out front. By the end of the first glass the wine has grown in stature. A delightfully subtle bouquet! Poured with a noble and generous hand! By the middle of the third glass they have become honorary Italians and the dusky air that surrounds them has become an expressive medium, to be shaped by gesturing arms. The line moves; they step over the threshold into a candlelit cavern filled with mayhem. The man behind the espresso machine heaves, grunts, yanks. A grey-haired woman in the kitchen is yelling. Our young Americans find themselves shoehorned like tardy picnickers into a communal table. A jug of red Chianti is thumped down; crusty bread fit for a peasant. Somebody fills their glasses from an open bottle. Three steaming bowls of minestrone appear, hunked with carrot and zucchini. Paul waxes poetic; Cynthia sips wine and leaves her soup untouched. Murray and Adele across the table are from San Diego by way of Brooklyn. Murray is wearing light blue polyester and puffing a cigar, roosterish behind big glasses. B-24 tail gunner during the war, shot down six times. Lousy planes used to run out of gas half a mile before you hit the runway. He squeezes Adele's hand; their tenth cruise—you name it, they've done it—and he's only seventy-eight going on fifteen. Quite a little life for a yeshiva kid from the Grand Concourse. He pours the youngsters another round. His jug is empty; Paul cracks open a fresh bottle and returns the favor. Extravagant toasts are exchanged. Prosciutto and melon follow, locally grown and cured. Did anybody say mouthwatering? Paul is on fire, McKay is delightfully trashed. Cynthia drinks and tries to smile. When the main course arrives, the young men swoon: two sizzling blackened bistecce fiorentini, each the size of a flattened calf. That's not steak! McKay cries. It's wooly mammoth! A party of three walks past the table; one of the men is a dwarf. See that guy? McKay whispers loudly. That's what happens when you drink too much of this wine. Feed him to the woolly mammoth! Paul shouts. Glasses are refilled, toasts invented. Adele wonders if New York is dangerous these days; such things you hear on the news! Nonsense, Murray barks: the place was always a nuthouse, knives if it wasn't guns. McKay worships at his steak for what seems like hours, sawing off hunk after tender hunk. Cynthia nibbles at her salad—mama's fresh cuttings—and makes the boys eat most of it. Vanilla ice cream for dessert, strawberries to die for. Murray hands out cigars.

The three young North Americans end up, much later, on the Ponte Vecchio. Cynthia has drunk too much and eaten too little. She leans over the balustrade and retches into the moonlit Arno. Paul and McKay steady her. The bridge is quiet and dark, the night warm and whirling. They walk Cynthia homeward along the river road like a war casualty, her arms thrown around their necks. She stumbles once and falls, knee to the curb; a large disheveled woman outlined in the glare of a dozen headlights. Past the Uffizi, David, Hercules. Her concierge has stepped out; they whisk her past the front desk, down the hall into her room. She collapses, dragging her saviors onto the bed. Paul strokes her arm, she rolls murmuring towards McKay. Time sags into collective stupor. McKay rouses himself and retreats to the bathroom, splashes, stares at the guy in the mirror. The guy in the mirror shakes his head No. Back on the bed, McKay is gentle but firm: he's tired, still healing and has to go home. Cynthia strokes his hand, moans wistfully. Paul comes to the rescue. Witching hour at La Tua Casa; fifteen more minutes and they'll be sleeping in the gutter. McKay gives her a kiss, then—after she rises laboriously—a hug. Paul clasps her hand. Of course they'll see her before they go. Then they're gone—out the front door of her pensione, chasing each other through darkened streets, breathless with hilarity and relief. Heading north tomorrow.

Found in Solingen

ontrol! sings the voice behind the door. A swift impatient rap. Passports!

Swimming on the slick surface of my naugahyde mattress, chilled under the single sheet. Climbing mountains all night. Then I'm flinging it off, awake, floundering for my money belt. Paul's doing the same on his side of the cabin.

Just a minute, I call out, ripping Velcro and unzipping. I leap down off the bunk and heave open the sliding door. Crouching a little in my underpants.

Two customs agents in military dress are standing in the hall outside our couchette, outlined in grey morning light.

Control, repeats the one in front, giving the word a cheerful rising-and-falling melody. Deutschland.

I hand him my passport. He flips through it, pausing. His partner leans in and looks around. I glance at Paul, who it also in underpants and has looked happier.

Danke schoen, the soldier says briskly, handing mine back as he takes Paul's.

Prego, I mumble.

Paul sighs. In this country we say bitte.

The second soldier mutters, then pulls out a flashlight and shines it at my Mouse on the bottom bunk. His partner glances at us, jerks his head. What is this device?

Would you like to explain or should I? Paul says dryly.

I, uh...musician, I say, pointing at my daypack as I move towards it. For making the music bigger. Harmonica. Blues.

They're both staring now. I unzip the outer pocket and pull out my A-harp, honk playfully, point at the Mouse. Big sound maker, I say, spreading my hands.

Big sound maker, echoes the first soldier, glancing at his partner as he hands back Paul's passport. Then he smiles and slaps the doorframe. Danke schoen, auf wiedersehen.

I stand in my underpants after they've gone, swaying with the train. We're flying along the edge of a twisting ravine. Overcast skies, a cool fall feel.

Welcome to the fatherland, Paul mutters. We hope your stay will be an enjoyable one.

We're sitting at a table in the dining car—five hours to Cologne—with menus open, the Rhine keeping pace like a flung grey scarf below our window. Heavy silver plate, real linen. Three or four castles so far, nestled among high pines at the craggiest, sharpest bends. The waiters are balding pros in maroon monkey jackets and speak half a dozen languages badly.

Breakfast seems to be reemerging as we head north, I say, staring at a hyper-real photo of waffles topped with cherries and whipped cream.

Paul sips water. I have a theory about this.

What the hell is Rumpfleisch? Filet of tailbone?

Would you like to hear my theory?

Does it involve scrambled eggs?

We should be so lucky.

I toss my menu on the table. I've always assumed you could trace the Industrial Revolution back to the introduction of coffee into Europe and the way time kept speeding up.

From goatherds to hackers in five hundred years.

Yeah, but see at that point you're really talking about a post-industrial sort of—

My theory.

Your theory.

Tiny breakfasts obtain among the meridional peoples—Italians, Spaniards, etcetera—because everybody gorges late at night because nobody feels like eating dinner at six because they're still waking up from the three-hour siesta they took after lunch, which was *also* huge because who wouldn't be starved by noon if all you'd had for breakfast was one lousy brioche and a gulp of bitter mud?

Did you say "meridional"?

His eyes are blazing behind his glasses. I've been waiting twenty-five years for the chance.

That's almost as bad as floccinaucinihilipilification.

Excuse me.

The act of estimating as worthless, I murmur, glancing up at our waiter. Longest word in the English language, except for pneumonoultramicroscopicsilicovolcanoconiosis. Do you know what you want?

Coffee, he sighs.

The waiter scribbles briskly. Eine kaffee....

Five minutes later we're making tea sandwiches of boiled ham and Muenster on black bread, clinking spoons on saucers. The brew is strong and good, almost winy. Little white pots of liverwurst and butter.

I lick my fingers and grin. High fat but what the fuck.

So die young, he shrugs, munching fastidiously.

Check it out, I say, nodding towards the window.

A clump of heads bobbing like golf balls in the river below. Two stooped older men in Speedo suits strap on bathing caps and wade in to join them: a swim club on excursion. Treading water, drifting slowly towards the shipping channel. Currents suddenly seize the leaders—stringing the pack downriver, scattering stragglers far behind. Mouths open in what seem like happy screams but we're too far away to tell.

Welcome to the Rhineland, Paul mutters.

I grab another piece of black bread. Looks like fun.

Hitler would certainly have approved.

Paul! I groan.

Look, he whispers, exasperated, I refuse to pretend I'm having a wonderful time when I am *not* having a wonderful time.

We've been in the country less than two hours.

His eye is brittle and unforgiving. I make no apologies for being a Jew.

Nobody's asking you to. Shit.

We stare into our cups, rocking gently with the train. My sugar packet says "sugar" in six languages, the last of which—squiggles and dots—looks like Arabic.

Midafternoon finds us heaving packs down onto one more anonymous railway platform—souls rising, hovering, flattening into a fragile surface like cream on milk. Paul cringes as stringent German voices drone arrival times out of overhead loudspeakers. We traipse through an underground corridor lit with ads for Granini apricot nectar, Drum tobacco. Der Denver-Clan! trumpets a poster: John Forsythe in a tux posed behind Linda Evans in diamonds—she's blonde, they've made it, America is swell—with Joan Collins lurking in the background, a double-breasted Dark Lady ready to pounce. Just past that is a starving Ethiopian, hand outstretched: Ein Tag Fur Afrika.

Marianna is waiting at a flower kiosk upstairs: a slim young woman in black boots and rhinestone-studded Hollywood starlet glasses, long black hair gashed with punkish blonde. Where's the baby fat I remember? The frantic schoolgirl? Her arms around my neck, a breathtaking hug, we're pulling away and inspecting. You've changed, McKay, she says with great moral seriousness. You're skinnier. Suddenly we're giggling. Would you like me to tell her why? the bearded Canadian asks. I'm not sure I would. He glares: because you've been running around Europe for the past three weeks like a chicken with its head cut off. Oooooh, Marianna pooh-poohs, I'm not believing this. Rubbing my shoulder. I've told her about Helen. Eyes searching mine, fierce and protective. A death in the family she refuses to accept.

Would we perhaps be interested to eat something tasty? Her voice is an indescribable train wreck of mother-tongue interference, lycée English wrestling with German and French—gargled vowels and tortured, barn-sized R's. She was knowing this pub just outside the Hauptbanhoff where we can get a real German snack. Kolsch, too. Koln-bier. This is how it's always being down through German history, you see—a thousand tiny villages, each isolated by geographic features, each madly jealous and mistrusting of strangers, each possessing a small-minded, violent prince brooding in his castle and a local-brewed beer. Were always becoming smashed before they made a raiding party on the next town over. You've heard of the barbarian hordes? Now we got Saturday football and the English boys are much worse.

The afternoon is cool and overcast, a season removed from Florence. Marianna nods at the huge blackened cathedral vaulting skyward. Funnily enough, the Kolner Dom was the only building not leveled by American bombs during the war. Everything else: poof! Because, of course, Uncle Sam's planes are using the pointy towers to locate Cologne from on top of the clouds. Then afterwards you got millions of GIs running through the streets being everybody's best friend, giving away cigarettes and building the ugly new shoeboxes we've been living with since fifty years like good little Germans.

The beer hall she takes us to looks like the sort of place Hitler could have made an early stir at. Three-quarters of the patrons are tourists, to judge from prevailing t-shirt logos. A couple of guys seated next to us are clanking tankards and calling each other dude. Somebody at the far end stands up and attempts to yodel; hands yank him down. Scattered hoots break out. Paul seems tense but stabilized. We're munching oversize hotdogs smeared with dark mustard, pulling at glasses of cold yeasty beer, each of which has a flawless head and a white paper collar identifying it as Kuppers. Marianna is wreathed in smoke, wrist arched. Is altogether incredible, this save-the-Africans business. You got one day last month set aside for a national holiday, every caritative organization and some specially invented by black marketers for the purpose were fanning out across Germany with coffee cans, slots in the top where you push your coins. Usually it's some famous movie star or sporting person shaking it at your face. Television cameras everywhere. And all the time announcers talking "Well, Holland raised fifty million deutschmarks last week, so we must raise at least one hundred million for starving Ethiopians." The Master Race! Spending all day in front of a TV watching good German people drop good German money into good German cans, everybody dizzy with good feeling. Next year they'll play Santa Claus one day for hungry indios in Brazil. Almost makes one fancy becoming Scrooge and shouting miserly things out loud so as not to lose one's mind.

Marianna has the waitress bring cafe au lait—kaffee mit schlagsahne—after lunch; ordering in her native tongue seems to reconstitute her as somebody harsh, demanding, distant. She was telling us about the family house in Solingen. More of a stone cottage, really; we shall feel quite as though someone's been tossing us back three hundred years into a fairy tale. Hot water presents a problem. Pity the poor damsel spending wintertimes there alone, nobody but ghosts to complain to! Wrinkling her mouth as she hands me the keys. Is altogether a frustration, having to say goodbye now for two days and disappear to Paris, but poor university students can't be choosy when the tourist office says Come work. Showing busfuls of American soldiers and their stupid blonde wives where the hunchback was hiding in Notre Dame Cathedral, then one beer at a cafe in Pigalle, making historical comments about Baron Haussman's sewage system while everybody's staring at sidewalk whores. Money is money; young geographers need to buy books.

Glancing at her watch, stubbing out her cigarette. Two minutes we've got before our bus. Her train leaves in eight. I notice Paul make a pained mental note about German efficiencies. Emerging from our beery cave to blink at the bright cloudy day. Hinged orange busses in a parking lot down below, a series of angled bays. Fresh breezes rake Paul's thinning hair; smoke lingers in Marianna's as we bend forward to brush cheeks. She's seeing us Tuesday afternoon for certain. Be friendly with the poltergeists!

Not one building but two: just off the highway, protected by chain-link fence overhung with vines. Marianna's mother is having the big house rebuilt to modern specifications. Paul and I creak through the unlocked gate, swing down crumbling slate steps into the stone cottage's shadow. A couple of chilled crickets chirping listlessly. The key she gave me fits; the wooden door sticks, fights, then swings smoothly inward past a jumble of mismatched rubber boots.

The bathroom downstairs has a toilet that holds your shit in full view—cupped in a shallow white indentation—until streaming waters hurl it over and away into the void. Suspended above the kitchen sink is a chrome hot-water heater shaped like a V-2 rocket. The living room upstairs—green velvet sofa, oriental rugs—would be comfy if we could get the electric heater to work. The white plastic coffee maker is a new Krups. Paul can't resist: old munitioneers don't die, they just retool. I'm familiar with Big Bertha? Seventy-seven mile range; a screaming comes across the Parisian sky courtesy of the Kaiser.

I fire the thing up—fragrant blup-blup—and we sit in our sweaters sipping good strong coffee from wide-lipped china cups, packs leaning against flower-papered walls. Neither of us has the heart to struggle with the coal stove. Pasturage rolls away from the back windows, dipping gently into a gully, rising towards a farmhouse clumped with pines on the crest.

Inertia threatens. We get up and stretch, then heave packs into facing bedrooms. Mine has two beds, one of which is piled high with a Salvation Army assortment of old blouses and dresses edged with lace. Goose-down comforter crumpled at the foot of the other. Paul calls out; I backpedal to find him thumbing at a snapshot tacked to the wall above Marianna's dresser. See anybody you know? I see Helen—ripping grin, dazed melting eyes—on one side and a cool, regal blonde named Maxine Duvel-Cohen on the other. Me in the middle, elbows around both necks. Last New Year's Eve.

Paul rummages on, grumbling about the weather. I am suspended between Helen's sensual gaze and the utter uselessness of the feelings it summons up. Cancerous lumps form at various nodes along my throat-core axis. For five years that smile was mine. Oh, Lonnie.

Ten minutes later Paul is off to town and I'm doing sprints up the dirt road behind the cottage. Quads are stiff but they warm up by the fifth or sixth repeat. The flock of goats grazing next to the farmhouse bleats every time I swoop past. The thing about hills—apart from building racing strength—was the way they focused the mind, burning off external distractions in a rush of vaporized glycogen. Half way up and your heart is on fire, controlled fission drifting towards meltdown. How hard you push determines how painfully you will die. Invisible ray guns are nuking your thighs; cold fusion byproducts prickle your fingertips. Only a hundred yards left. You will make a beautiful corpse. The billy goat gods are waiting, jaws tensed.

Back at the cottage I stagger around the bathroom. No hot water? I'll be an animal. Stripping off my shorts as the faucet roars, a dipped toe and I'm suddenly made aware of the crucial distinction between tolerably cool and bracingly icy. Subterranean springs are involved.

I'm toweling off in the living room and humming when Paul bangs through the front door. He drops groceries in the kitchen, plods up the steps. He could hear my screams a hundred yards up

the street. This merely confirmed his first impression of the neighbor-
hood. No he is not in a good mood. Welcome to Solingen, birthplace
of—would you believe?—Adolf Eichmann. Not that the local book-
store particularly cares whether visiting Jews might take offense at a
"scholarly" window-display featuring their favorite son. We quiet our
heart, say a prayer for Hannah Arendt and move on. We pass storefront after storefront filled with stainless-steel kitchen knives, hunting knives, daggers, scissors, and nail clippers. Did we know before
we accepted our host's invitation that stainless-steel instruments
of torture were the town's primary industry? We ignore our better
instincts and go shopping. Foodstuffs are purchased at a local super-
market without incident, even though it's painfully obvious that the
old woman on checkout line watching us fumble through our change
is thinking *Jew!* Horns included at no extra charge. Little do we
know what awaits at the local bread shop. One would have thought
that our meager attempts at simulating German through a combi-
nation of remembered Yiddish exclamations—thank you, Grandma
Goldberg—and expressive shrugs would have been met with at least
moderate forbearance, if not outright warmth. And God is a chicken
with nothing better to do than sit on your eggs.

Nightmare. One moment he's politely trying to find out the difference between Vitalbrotchen and Zweibelbrotchen, the next a store-
ful of tightlipped old women is staring at him as though the Antichrist
has descended. Through the front door hobbles Grandfather Hans in
a brand of green Tyrolean hat favored by German military exiles in
certain sections of suburban Paraguay. The women greet Hans, Hans
greets them. One big happy family. Everybody is somehow managing
to eye the bearded Jew and ignore him at the same time. The woman
behind the counter has moved on to the next order. She is giving the
bearded Jew more time to make up his mind, perhaps? She drops a

loaf of brown bread in a slicer on the counter and flicks the switch. A flurry of stainless-steel blades. The bearded Jew needs no more time.

The coil heater is glowing like an old toaster; Marianna's dusty record player is recycling Louis Armstrong's Greatest. Dinner was stir fry chicken with Westphalian vegetables—cabbage, celery—washed down with sweet Rhine wine. The living room is cozy with the front drapes pulled so we can't hear Porches whizzing by. Farmhouse floodlights cutting tiny swaths in the blackness out back. We're trading war stories.

I had no idea the whole thing was that sexual, I say, setting down my glass.

Sexual? he hoots. McKay, the woman was demonic.

Different positions, the whole—

Whips and chains, handcuffs....

Get outta here....

He's patting air, calming me. No handcuffs.

Stop...in the naaaaame of love.

Love had nothing to do with it. He's gazing at the ceiling, palms spread in benediction. Armstrong's notes pulse with the wine we've drunk. A new word must be invented, he sighs.

Total bodily need.

Total and complete bodily need to the point of systemic nervous collapse when the woman suddenly and mysteriously decides that you are no longer to be the perpetual beneficiary of the beast with two backs.

The bottle is in my hand as we slap.

Wreck does not begin to describe what I was.

I remember you were like totally broken up when the whole thing crashed and burned.

He sips, thinks, then lifts his glass: 'A pour'd a flagon of Rhenish on my head once. This same skull, sir, was, sir, Yorick's skull, the King's jester.

Let's hear it for the jester.

My kingdom for a horse.

Hiyo Hamlet.

Egglet. Piglet.

Wind in the Willows.

Women! he cries.

Don't do it! You're making a terrible mistake!

Judith, he sighs.

We sit, silent. Louis is nailing his blistering cadenza intro to "Basin Street Blues."

Well, I finally say, I'm sorry you can't stay.

So am I.

What are you gonna do without me in Amsterdam?

Rembrandt and Van Gogh.

The Heineken Factory Tour is supposed to be interesting.

So are the drugs and the brothels, which doesn't necessarily mean I'll do either.

Come on, live a little.

I think we've been doing quite well at that, actually.

We certainly did Florence.

I thought her name was Cynthia.

Fuck.

Take your head out of your hands, young man.

Now look, I say, when I show up at the pensione in Paris on... what day did we say? July....

July 3rd. Nine days.

When I show up on July 3rd I don't want the gypsy woman and her boys coming after me with scimitars telling me Meeeester Goldbeerg have stay two day and runs off without he paya the bill.

Would I do a thing like that? he says meekly.

I'll kill you.

Back to the gypsy womaaaaan! he yells, raising his glass.

The house gets quiet later when we turn off the record player. Splashed on my face, cold water downstairs seems drawn from impossibly deep wells. I bump past Paul on my way back up; two guys sporting t-shirts, underpants, hairy bare legs. No top sheet so I pull the goose-down comforter up to my chin. Paul calls out; he'll wake me at seven-thirty, an hour before his bus. I hear him banging around, rustling, sighing. My bedroom window is open. It's a peaceful night.

The Knots

"By passion the world is bound
by passion too it is released"

The Hevajra Tantra

As my hands eclipse

your skin

light presses

deep into my bones.

A corona

streams upward

with earthsick fire

lighting my fingers

a molten red.

Entering you

I am lost

among the archipelagoes

of your breasts

as we unbind

the world's knots.

Tornado kisses

litter the bed

with the shells

of broken forms.

Eyes pummel

the sky

with blue chisels.

A flick of your thigh

sends walls flying.

Air rips

      with pounding

and I am drowning

 drowning in heat

until we give

      a final clap

that resolves

      into white space

and there is only Time

    slowly retying knots

with breathing string.

Paul Goldberg
June 198-
Firenze

He's left *The Divine Comedy* on Marianna's night table. I discover it when I get back upstairs after our awkward roadside hug, diesel fumes lingering in my nostrils. Pages cleaved by a black Bic fine-point and a new poem: goodbye purgatory, hello paradise. I steal his pen, slap the book closed, toss it on the living room table. The moment I stop moving the house gets too quiet. Unhooking latches, throwing open bay windows—starlings screaming in the morning chill, a twenty-foot drop to gravel below. I pull my head back inside. Quads aching from yesterday's hill repeats; the incline looks gentler at this distance, grey ribbon floating towards the fogged crest.

I am sitting on Marianna's sofa with my old journal—stained, filled, spine wrenched—at my hip and the new one in my lap, sipping coffee. Starting fresh. Pen poised; it's a thinner, scratchier line than my hemorrhaged blue medium-point. Flipping open the back cover of #1: Bill Grant c/o Mr. and Mrs. Wiliam L. Grant Sr., 459 W. Sycamore Dr., Carbondale, IL 44113. That dream *did* happen. You didn't make it all up.

I push the story forward—all-night sail through the Swiss Alps in the bowels of a swaying couchette—until my hand cramps. The living room seems empty without Paul. I switch on the small new television next to the desk. MTV, EuroSport, couple of German soaps. I stare at rapidly intercut images of beautiful mulatto models and smoke-wreathed blond guitar gods gyrating to computer-generated drumbeats, then flick the remote and watch torpedo-shaped motorcycles hurtling around curves bill-boarded with petroleum brand names, then flick back and forth until I'm filled with a generalized desire to fuck, consume, and hurl myself into the void. At least the Germans live in real time and care about something. I watch them scheme and rage—entranced by their passionate harshness, not understanding a word.

I stumble across Ero-Scope as I'm trying to turn the thing off. French programming: a live broadcast from the terrace of a beach-front hotel in Cannes. Host Jean-Pierre is young, tan, brash, smooth, gorgeous; his female cohost Natalie, mid-thirtyish, has gained in character what she's lost in looks. They're joined by Camus—older, olive-skinned, glistening smile—who is in charge of interviewing the three girls. First stage of competition is called Maxi: vogueing down the boardwalk in skirts and tight t-shirts. Dr. Livingstone's little island is a fleeting blur over their shoulders. Both white girls are conventionally sexy; the girl from Cameroon is a vision of paradise. Lidded eyes, heart-shaped face, lips pillowed with gentleness and intelligence. She parries Camus' suggestive questions with frankness and good humor. Radiant grin; take away the chestnut skin and she's Helen's twin. Jean-Pierre and Natalie banter approvingly; a pan-European straw poll is taken, viewers calling a toll-free number with preferences. She's neck-and-neck with Miss Valois. Second stage of the competition is Mini: one-piece maillots. Behold the treasures of West Africa. Where was she when I was down there? Europe's voting heart agrees with me. Third Stage is Seduction: sitting across a table from Camus and telling him your ideal date, what you'd like to do to him at the end of the night, etcetera. The two white girls are more than game; his eyes crinkle with laughter, astonishment, and precum. Super! exclaims Jean-Pierre, encouraging onlooker applause. Miss Cameroon sits, quivering with life; Camus basks in her glow. The ebony princess. What does she have in store? She takes his hand. Crooning a French lullaby—eyes melting, locked on his. He tries to chuckle his way out and can't. She's for real. Won't stop. His eyes go liquid, his head drops. The crowd roars; Jean-Pierre and Natalie exclaim. Annihilation!

I'm sitting cross-legged on the Persian carpet in the middle of Diana's living room with a pliers and my Mouse. Unscrew four bolts and the speaker frame pulls away from the hole. The black paper cone is dry, powdered with brine crystals. I touch the jagged flap where my finger punched through on that hopeless morning in Cannes. You can almost hear Bill awshucksing. I lean down, sniff. Topless girls lolling on hot soft sand; I'm plunging sunblind into surf, heart wine-blown. Sing me a siren song of the sweet summer south.

Nothing but a low hum when I plug in my mike. Dead batteries? I bolt the thing carefully back together, my soul strangely light. Bill would chuck the electronics, stretch skin over the hole and make a drum. Leaping up, I'm suddenly dancing around the room—a crazed fool has taken possession, he's hooting, heeeeyaaaaahing, making faces in the hall mirror. Icy water from the downstairs sink makes me shudder with delight. Heaving open the front door, I can smell moss, humus, the damp low places where toads hide out. Dog barking in the distance. I howl back.

Marianna wakes me early the following evening, shouldering through the front door downstairs. I've been dozing all day except for a couple of harp-blowing fits and the supply run into town. Granini Aprikose Nektar, six-pack of Kuppers Kolsch. Vital fluids have been replenished, lingering virii put to rout; Rip Van Winkle stretches like a jungle cat, swimming in the delicious languor of nowhere he has to be. She flicks on a light, leans down to brush my cheeks, collapses in a chair. Groans.

The cup of coffee she hands me a few minutes later is my first since Monday morning and very strong. She manhandles the Krups—filter paper, grounds, bulky inserted plastic body—with something verging on racial pride. Two years now she's been leading trips to Paris and it's getting enough; one spends so many hours rushing to and fro on trains one quite forgets where one is. Eighty-seven American soldiers with wives, screaming brats for kids. Time for a pit stop! Invading forces piling out of motor coaches, all the men possess this same scrubbed-toothpaste smile. Ten-four on the frog brewskies, good buddy! She pities the poor frantic garcons. Claps her hands and yells after a couple of rounds, they're piling back on board, saluting through the windows, yeehawing like cowboys. Everybody buys horrid plastic Eiffel Towers after making sheep eyes at the real thing; two brats stick each other like duelists, one screams Ow! Utter madness to think history lessons might be communicated under such circumstances. One does one's job, collects one's pay and Pfffft! Home.

She's terribly sorry for Paul but can't blame him; wishes only he'd been staying long enough to know the story of her maternal grandfather rebelling the Nazis. Her Algerian father fighting the French! A racialist's nightmare she is, truly; she'd have been among the first to be gassed. No easy task proving oneself an Aryan back then, even if you were a Norse god. New laws made an essentially impossible requirement for certifying papers; no Jewish blood allowed after 1715. Her grandfather took his revenge on these idiots. Editor-in-chief of Zie Solingener Zietung, Herr Bacharach would receive weekly emissions from Goebbels informing him the true—disastrous—situation of the German military, added with a small paragraph of purest propaganda about thrilling triumphs and other idiocies that he must only print on Page One. This he did, in quotation marks, with cynical commentaries underneath. Threats naturally thundered down from the war gods in Berlin: a man with four children could misplace one very easily, we'll pay you a free vacation in scenic Buchenwald. Deafness in the face of barking dogs was always a Bacharach weakness; in January 1944 he was writing a final headline accusing the Nazis as suicidal madmen, recommending further that Germany must surrender immediately. Then poof! Gone. Only his family was remaining when soldiers banged rifle butts against the house next door. A crazy idiot! yelled his wife. No idea where he's gone! And anyway we've not been making love since five years! The soldiers cringed; six months later the Reich expired and she was joining him—future beloved mayor—in Dinkelsbuhl, Bavaria.

But what about Helen? Marianna won't let me rest until I've told all; a vein of emotion plays at my vocal cords, fingers threatening to strangle me suddenly torn loose. Yes I hurt. No language for describing how close we were, before things fell apart. Bodies beaten to sobs, a tingling starfall, sea-green foam lapping at smooth sand. Sweet stirring of limbs, hours later. Now it's all gone. Marianna's leaning forward to stub out her hand-rolled butt; all the truest things make for extreme difficultness in telling. It's the difference among newspapers and poems. At the same moment she's knowing from Helen's letters how deeply I'm cared for. Perhaps love is an allowing of confusion, struggle, growth. Makes no sense to depressedly insist on final endings unless one's talking about death. Whatever freedom Helen grasps is also, in this sense, my own. Speaking of life: am I capable of interesting myself in beers at an alternative pub?

It's pleasantly cool outside as we bump shoulders along the highway leading to town. Occasionally a faint buzz blossoms, swells as driving lights sweep into view—a Porche or Mercedes with third gear hammered, blowing past and disappearing around the bend like a slot car clinging to grooved track. Every house we pass is hedged with chain-link fence. Marianna raises her arm to point out Orion, three pinpoints twinkling against blue-black sky. She's been one time at night in the Sahara, two hundred kilometers south of Algiers; so many stars pressing down one's afraid of becoming crushed.

Soon we're thumping up the steps of a gabled Victorian house at the crest of a long hill. Marianna welcomes me to the Liederkiste as we push inward; I'm steeled for nose rings, black leather, polymorphous perversity. The front room—white lace curtains, scattered bridge tables—is empty except for a skinny guy with long wispy prophet's beard and John Lennon glasses hovering behind the bar. Friedrich! Marianna cries. His eyes rise from three tumblers of beer he's drawing; take her in warmly; fall as she chatters and he works on, inch by golden inch with pauses to let the heads settle. A poster tacked to the wall behind me: stylized white dove superimposed on a mushroom cloud; KEINE NEUEN ATOMRAKETEN. We follow Friedrich into the back room and grab a table as he floats off. There's a battered piano on the empty stage; Cream's "Strange Brew" boom-boom-thwacks out of twin loudspeakers, mingling with scattered low murmurs. Two girls in green U.S. Army jackets are sofa-lounging next to a young Turk, basking in his smile.

I'm savoring my first kolsch—stringent brewing laws, no impurities—when Marianna returns from the toilet with two friends. Teddy is burly, has kind eyes, plump reddened lips, a scrabbly goatee. He eases himself into a chair, revealing Rikki. Rikki nods, barely seeing me as she sits, tosses her green fedora onto the table, shakes long black plaits out of her face—a slim young black woman in a baggy grey sweater—and gazes furiously at the candle, nose flaring, cheeks flickering bronze. Feathered silver earring dangling from one lobe. Death and destruction rain as she turns and hemorrhages German at Marianna, a sustained machine-gun burst directed at unseen antagonists. I stare at her pearly teeth—understanding nothing, feeling everything. She mimics, mocks, rages; pushes up her sleeves to reveal astonishing forearms, tendons jumping under satiny brown skin. Marianna clucks with concern. Friedrich floats into view with another round. Rikkiiii, murmurs Teddy, rubbing her hand. She gulps half a glass, flashes reddened eyes at me, then buries her head and begins to sob. Marianna rubs her back and leans towards me; is a terrible thing, really. Not only does her boyfriend make love with other girls but yesterday he tells her I'm getting sick from all you Germans, I think next week I'll go home to Italia.

Dinner comes—vegetarian lasagna, spinach salad—and more tall flawlessly headed beers. Rikki cheers up enough to nibble. I watch her lips bunch as she pops an olive, works it with teeth and tongue, then pushes out the pit and lays it gently on her plate. She's a dancer; notices me for the first time when Marianna translates my question. Her gaze is skeptical and amused. Donkey show, she mimics when I thank Teddy for passing the salad. Hands shaking as she lights up and suddenly she's raging again, a torrent of aggrieved love. Friedrich floats up, sets down another round and floats away; Janis Joplin is squalling faintly through the smoky haze. Time glides by. Teddy has disappeared with a parting hug, Marianna—we've exchanged confidences—has discovered friends at another table. Rikki and I are facing each other, flung into a charmed clearing, desperately trying to make ourselves understood. Heartbreak! Commitment! The madness of lovers! She speaks little English but nods at mine, squirming with frustration when her German response draws a blank. French and Italian words flutter between us like trading cards; meanings collapse, we chuckle at sounds. My heart jumps every time her forearms ripple. She draws on a cigarette with head cocked and plaits dangling, eyes narrowed, gazing at me. I finger her green fedora, then model it and pout like Mick Jagger; an explosion of laughter—borderline sob— and she's touching my hand, holding it, squeezing. Our eyes lock. The wells in this country are dizzyingly deep.

Marianna returns, insisting Rikki stay the night with us so as not to cry alone; a swirl of coat-grabbing and we're tumbling into a Mercedes taxi out front. Rikki and I slouch in back, shoulders bumping around high-speed curves. Stroking her hand, brushing my lips against her slippery plaits. She turns, enervated, and makes me understand in German-Franglais creole that she's not the kind of girl who meets a man one night and goes pfft. I cluck, murmur. Roadside fences flicker by like unfurled chainmail armor.

We pile out of the car at Marianna's. A discussion ensues between women as we float down the walkway into cool fragrant darkness, guided by crickets. Rikki's wearing jeans and work boots, daypack shoulder-slung. Marianna translates as we pause, shadowed by the big empty house next to the cottage: three weeks since we've been having a dancing party upstairs, seems our guest is seriously crazy to make a revisit. Shrugging, she pushes through the unlocked door, flicks her disposable lighter in the darkness—root-cellar damp, pungent with pine—and guides us up stone steps through a skeleton doorway into a large unlit space. We catch our breath, faces flickering. Ghetto-blaster perched on sawhorses, scattered beer cans, candles melted onto a sheetrock table. Vague reek of pot. Next moment Rikki has popped in her own cassette and is whirling into the shadows, oblivious; I've sagged back on a milk-crate. Marianna's yawning as she hands me a lighter: she's going to bed and very much hopes I'll not start any fires. Tchuss!

I sit like the Statue of Liberty until my fingers burn, then light two candle butts and stand awkwardly, embarrassed for staring, devouring every move. Rikki's hips gyrate like jeweled bearings; the fluidity and snap defy words. I sway in place—wanting to join in, embarrassed by my incompetence. Her work boots edge and hop; the shiver in her shoulders pushes into my throat. Clenched brown fists as she hurls into a turn, stops, looks both ways, falls backward onto one splayed hand, reaches for the sky, legs bowed, pelvis heaving.

Her panting is the only sound when the tape clicks off. Wobbling towards me stiff-kneed, hands on hips, she grins shyly at my praise. Crouches grey-sweatered to zip her pack: a self-contained, tight-bodied little animal.

We blow out candles, navigate the darkened maze leading out the back door, across the yard and upstairs. Marianna's bedroom door is closed. Rikki glances at the living room sofa, me. I nod at my bedroom and mumble: two beds, I'm sleeping in there. She leans in, sniffs the cool heaviness of fluffed goose down, then shrugs and drops her daypack on my bed.

I close the door. She folds her arms and stares defiantly at me. The far bed is heaped with old dresses, blankets, folded sweaters. I reach across, gather, and heave everything onto the floor. Sneering, she removes her feathered silver earring and sets it on the headboard, kicks off her boots, strips off her jeans—smoothness of brown thighs below white panties—and climbs into my bed, pulling the comforter up to her chin. Reaches out and sets her daypack on the floor. I strip off my jeans and climb over her, collapsing onto the far bed, snuggling under the comforter's unclaimed half.

I lie motionless, staring at the ceiling. The room is bathed in silvery light from the unshaded window. Silent except for my heart. A soft rustle and her hand suddenly curls into mine, burrowing. Lifting my head; her face is turned away.

Our fingers nuzzle, arch, frolic like dolphins in a tropical lagoon. The rest of her lies frozen. A silent fevered hour passes. The hand I've been making love to could not be more responsive, its possessor more absentee. Bladder screaming, I finally let go and leap out of bed, pad barefoot down stone steps, take an endless angled sitting piss, and fly north to resume. Knuckles brushing her palm; caressing, squeezing, aching.

Rikki, I whisper hoarsely. A plea stammered in three languages; unmistakable blues edge.

Another half hour and she's drifted into my arms, bare legs draped over mine. I'm nuzzling her neck, swooning in a perfumed tangle of plaits and dusky curved jawline. Her face is still averted. My patience knows no limits. Hands gliding across her thighs and calves, shying away from the rest. Her belly under a fingered edge of fluffed sweater is satiny and firm. She shivers, says nothing. Withdrawing, I brush a hand lightly across her parted lips. She nuzzles my palm.

An eternity later she's licking it and moaning. We still haven't kissed. I've died a thousand deaths; all roads lead towards the sacred grove and may be booby-trapped. Relaxing my embrace, falling back. The ceiling is luminous with reflected starglow. I lean in and peck her cheek for no good reason. She whirls suddenly, seizing my head—wide-eyed, nostrils flaring—and crushes her lips against mine, groaning, breath pushing into my throat. Murmurs my name so I can feel it everywhere. She's all muscle and bone; could tear me apart. The comforter slides off as we roll.

B reakfast is in the living room, midafternoon.
Rikki sits in a green velvet chair—one leg folded, one dangling—and watches me, sipping coffee. Marianna bustles. I
spread pale firm butter on chewy brown bread, lop off a schmear of
liverwurst. George Benson is soloing on the stereo: every guitar-note
doubled with scatted voice, like dancers chasing each other's shadows.

Where's the sun? Still cloudy out, grey, autumnal. We're squir-
rels huddling in fluffed sweaters.

The olives are from Greece, courtesy of Aunt Gerta. Marianna
heaves the big jar up from downstairs. Huge, purple, spicy; blurbling
in a sour green sea of virgin olive oil, vinegar, lemon slices, and bay
leaves. Dip one out with a long-handled wooden spoon, pop it, lick
your fingers. Odysseus never had it so nice.

A hunk of pale orange Edam, smoked ham like thick-sliced
prosciutto.

The Krups sighs when the second pot is finished brewing.
Marianna pours. Wide-lipped china cups rimmed with gold, matching saucers. The stuff warms me as it slides down.

Rikki picks her teeth with a pinky, draws on a cigarette and
exhales.

My feet are cozy in yesterday's socks.

Marianna was just telling us about a voyage she's made to Egypt this past winter with Armud, her German stepfather. He's utterly deaf unless you shout. No such thing as window-shopping in Cairo; dare even to glance at a display and the owner insists you join him inside for tea—no matter if you're not buying, we're all friends. Pharaoh's empire was five miles wide and six hundred miles long: a straight line through the desert. Floods every year insuring fertility.

Rikki gazes levelly at me, like a cat. Murmurs something in German as I pop another olive and gaze back. Marianna answers and they both laugh.

She likes you, Marianna says.

Rikki makes a face, sticks out her tongue at me.

I'm happy, I say. Oil dribbling down my chin. I wipe with my hand, smearing.

Later, before dinner, I fill a pot with hot water and take a sponge bath downstairs. Marianna and Rikki are smoking at the kitchen table; their words hiss and rasp in a comforting rhythm. The tile floor is chilly against my bare feet. Rikki reaches an arm between my legs and hugs a thigh without looking up. Steam rises as I heave the pot into the bathroom, kicking the door closed. Strip jay-naked, crouch on cold plastic. The guy in the mirror has tousled hair and a hard-on. I'm whistling as I heave the steaming pot up into Marianna's old zinc tub, grab soap and a washcloth and get to work. An ice-cold rinse raises gooseflesh; I strangle my screams and feel wild.

Marianna translates Rikki's story later while I'm sitting at the table cutting up carrots and celery for soup. Rikki eyes me with wary bemusement, sips wine through rosebud lips. She's hardly knowing her father; died when she was three. Naturally one's neighbors manufactured a scandal—white woman with brown baby!—but sculptresses have no time to worry about stupid shit. Her mother was already an ethnic catastrophe, having been born in Lima, Peru with mixed bloods from Spaniards, Germans, Japonaise, and Inca chiefs. Nevertheless upraised to be a Good German—schools, holidays, national anthem—with bourgeois behaviors. All this ends at twenty-one when she flies to Hamburg on summer holiday and discovers bohemia. Jazz, nightclubs, everybody's a starving painter or writer. When September arrives she sells the homeward ticket and defects. Meets Rikki's father after two years, serving him drinks in a club where she's working to pay for jewelry materials. This exceedingly black man in U.S. Air Force costume smiles and says Hey darlin', w'at's dat pretty lil t'ing hangin' roun' ya neck? She explains how she's making art from hammering silver together with pieces of junk found in garbage dumps. His fingers are long and dark; a Trinidader from Philadelphia who parachutes from planes. His name was Lucien Sample. Six months later they're married, Rikki comes along five months after that. Lucien is madly prideful, installing his new family at the military dormitory; thinking perhaps when servitude concludes he'll transport everybody home to the islands, build a wood house—she'll help hammer nails—and open a restaurant. He loves to cook, especially fish. The women love his cooking. Everything is beautiful until the parachute doesn't open one day and he hits the ground and dies. Frau Sample starts making her big sculptures—twisted bedsprings, wrecked car parts—after that. Rikki was elevated mostly in Berlin, spending summers near Sienna because the pink marble was cheap.

Dinner is soup and orange pan bread which refuses to rise and we're forced to stir omelette-like into a soggy delicious mess.

Marianna apologizes for the gas oven; poltergeists at work. We dine by candlelight using big spoons. The sweet Rhine wine goes with everything. My fingers brush Rikki's cheek as I admire her feathered earring. Marianna is suddenly thundering about the folly of animal-liberty fascists who would not only forbid all human usage of imperiled-species furs—a reasonable program—but seem determined to impose their sentimentalized and hopelessly Western form of militant vegetarianism on indigenous peoples who would greatly prefer to roast a suckling pig on feast day and garland themselves with the eyeteeth of Cousin Wolf. Nature does not weep when the lion ravages the wilderbeest. Which is not to say that one should watch idly as malicious boys torture a kitten; just to recognize that this same kitten, given the chance, might torture a mouse with fully as much maliciousness. Why should we shame of being animals? Civilization requires an acknowledgment and constructive elaboration of this fact, not an ostrich-like burying of one's head.

Dessert is strawberry shortcake: Rikki hulls and slices with the big tarnished knife while Marianna and I take turns whipping. Vanilla extract, sugar, a splash of brandy. No grownups around to frown at obscenely huge dollops. Rikki and I play footsie as we gorge; she licks her finger suggestively, stares icily when I do the same, kicks me when I turn towards Marianna, yelps when I grab her under the table. We're holding hands as Marianna and she rattle on. Candles flicker; one sputters, dies. Hobgoblin shadows loom behind us, dancing on the walls.

When Marianna blows out the last candle we all scream, then giggle hysterically, find each other's hands, bump chairs away from the table and stand up. A chain forms—my hands resting on Marianna's hips, Rikki's floating on my shoulders. Rikki nuzzles my neck as we flow towards the stairs; I reach back and shove a hand down her jeans, flattening my fingers against her sweet, twitching ass.

The next morning is bright, blowy, fresh. Thursday, according to Marianna; I've misplaced my watch.

We catch a bus out to the Bergisches Castle after breakfast. Rikki's wearing my Panama hat and draws stares which she ignores. It feels strange to be carrying my Mouse—relic from another life—but there's no place to stow it before we meet Friedrich at his shop.

The bus winds through scattered hamlets nestled in foothills, gingerbread pubs beckoning with neogothic calligraphy: Kuppers, Furftenburg, Dinkel Acker. We get off on a small bridge lined with bursting flowerboxes next to a sign reading Wupper. The river below is window-glass green, foaming white over rocks, smoothing to a dappled sheen where the ski lift crosses and slants uphill. Marianna squints through rhinestone-studded glasses and points out our destination, squatting at the summit behind pointed firs.

His name was Engelbert Graf Von Berg. We stand in the small courtyard with blockhouses rising around us and stare at bulking tarnished bronze, fluffy white clouds scudding overhead. The helmet and chainmail must have weighed down his horse. Forty was a ripe old age back then.

The weapons are inside, on the museum's second floor. I'd never realized spears came tipped with so many different heads. The swords are all grey and must weigh forty pounds each. Rapiers, crossbows, muskets; a powder horn inlaid with ivory. A display case in the last room marked Madonna Mit Kind - 1300. She has no right arm, he's missing both.

Rikki takes my hand as we stroll downhill towards the bus stop; I squeeze back. A white-haired couple working their way uphill stare—or do they?—and my heart falters, then fills. I lift her hand to my lips and lose myself in the softness of brown skin, her skin, her, my Rikki.

The bus arrives precisely at the posted time, according to Marianna's watch. My amazement amuses them.

The Liederkiste is hedged with rhododendrons and looks distinctly suburban by day. Friedrich is inventorying liquor levels as we push through the front door. Of course he remembers me; his eyes glow softly behind rimless spectacles. Long wispy beard, black Chinese slippers. He glides wraithlike into the kitchen and I follow as the women linger, lighting up cigarettes over Cokes.

His basement shop is immaculate and well lit, rows of boxed vintage tubes—GE, RCA—stacked under an emerald Yes poster, air sweet with solder flux. We bench my Mouse, unbolt the grill. He nods knowingly at the ravaged speaker-cone: two years he was working at this music shop in Minneapolis, every month Prince's bass player brought in the same Gallien-Kreuger cabinet with blown voice coils.

He touches the needles of his voltmeter to various silvery nodes on the printed circuit board like an acupuncturist probing meridians. Battery voltage is slightly low; a trickle charge will fix that. He picks a greenish-black fleck off two solder nubs and hands it to me: never a good concept, mixing seaweed with electronic components.

Would I like tea? Bubbles gather on the immersion coil as he reaches onto a shelf for bags and sugar.

I've been retrofitted with an antique classic: six-inch Jensen horn pulled from a gutted '55 Fender Champ. Alnico magnet, now perfectly aged. He rebolts as I toss back sweet tannic dregs and unzip my daypack, pull out my mike and harps.

The sound is sweet, punchy, yawping, me; we've landed in Oz, color blossoming everywhere. There's the yellow brick road.

Flying Home

I caught a bus to Cologne Friday morning after breakfast. It was time to go. I made Rikki keep my Panama hat. She looked like a Sea Island Geechee woman, straw brim flaring down over black plaits. She pulled a button off her daypack and pinned it to my t-shirt: DON'T WORRY, BE HAPPY. She and Marianna walked me out to the road. Balmy breezes tickled my arms; fields of green wheat swayed stiffly in the sun. Sports sedans vroomed by, Doppler-shifting as they passed. It felt like summer again. Nobody said anything. I kissed Marianna on both cheeks as the bus rolled to a punctual stop. Things suddenly smeared and got very bright. The hat tumbled off Rikki's head as I grabbed her—tenderly, our lips brushing—and spun away, heaving myself onto the bus. Tchuss! cried Marianna, waving. I watched them shrink and shrink and finally disappear.

I took a train to Amsterdam and spent three days out of the five I had left. Centraal Station was plastered with "Beware of Pickpockets" signs. It was HomoWeek, according to posters; several men on the trolley into town had mustaches dyed bright pink. All the young men without mustaches looked like speedskaters, strapping and blond.

The Dutch way with draft beer is different from the German: slosh the glass full and slap off excess foam with a plastic slapper. Draft Heineken in Amsterdam is Van Gogh on a starry night. I got Van Goghed at the Maloe Melo watching a rockabilly quartet named The Wildcats entertain a roomful of fans who also had greased Elvis hair. You couldn't tell anybody was Dutch until "Jailhouse Rock" was over and the lead singer gargled his thanks. Two Lebanese ran the shawarma stand on Niewe Prinsengracht where I wolfed down a pita stuffed with lamb chunks drizzled with hot red oil, fingers licked after every bite. Pausing on a humped bridge under a poet's moon, cool green water fanning through radiating canals. No imperial sightlines in this city. Two Petty Officers from the British Navy in a Red Light District bar told me how six mates had gotten pissed inshore the night before and heaved some poor wanker's Citroen over the edge. Dutch bobbies threw a fit; had to ring up three canal tugs, helicopters with spots. We walked down the block past windows lit with dull red bulbs in which women in scanty undergarments were lounging on divans. A voluptuous black vixen with painted lips winked at me. John and Buck made randy comments; I drifted away, depressed. Breakfast the next morning at Bob's Youth Hostel was piles of scrambled eggs, toast, and coffee in the crammed low front room, white kids with dreads wreathed in spicy hash smoke. I hung with Jake, my bunkmate from Santa Monica who'd hooked up with a girl from the Bulldog Cafe his first night in town. Five kinds of grass on the menu. We sat on a bench across from the Anne Frank House and devoured a loaf of fresh raisin bread smeared with sweet butter. Old men smoking cigars whirred past on balloon-tired bicycles. I jammed later in front of Centraal Station with a Surinamese kid named Haj— wraparound shades, headband—who played his Japanese Strat left-handed, like Hendrix. The Bottom Stompers we weren't but "Voodoo

Chile" drew a crowd. Somebody handed me a large brown bottle of Heineken as I was unplugging, yeasty froth filling the neck. Who needed a hat? The trip suddenly felt like a success.

I started missing Rikki, walking back to Bob's. A trolley grinding around a curve almost flattened me. I stayed in after dinner. Our dorm room filled: two black girls in butter-yellow dresses from St. Lucia; three Italian girls; an unshaven stoned Greek heaving an Air Jordan duffle bag; and an elderly Frenchwoman with bad makeup. Everybody tried to be discreet. One Italian girl offered me a plum. They were from Lucca. Lots of shifting and sighing after lights out. The old Frenchwoman mumbled in her sleep. Allons enfants! La croix de la guerre!

I was up early, packed and plunging into the foggy morning. An old white man with Hemingway's beard was playing bottleneck blues on the Dam Rak as I flew by. A starling swarm filled the sky in front of Centraal Station, swooped down on a helpless tree, made it boil with frantic chirps. Pushing through the front doors I was stopped by a young guy—goatee and mustache, reddish lips—who radiated delighted gentleness and knew what my Mouse was for. Always in Copenhagen he was wanting to buy this one. Conservatory student moonlighting in long-distance car delivery; Antwerp-Nancy this afternoon. He popped open his guitar case to show me his sunburst Guild. Soon we were bouncing towards our gate, fates fused for a day. His name was Nils. He went off to fetch coffees from the dining car while I splayed myself across four seats to keep our six-person cabin ours. Thick beige kafeemilch, cinnamon-dusted crackers. Our groove was natural and could have achieved world domination if we'd met four weeks earlier. Windmills flashed by, baking-sheet flatness of Holland rumpling into low Belgian hills. Centraal Station in Antwerp was a swirl of black-suited Hasidim clutching invisible diamonds. We bought a paper tray of hot sizzling frites and wandered into the warmish smudged noon, munching. Nils smiled; last time he's coming in this city he makes a mistake with drinking three Duvel beers, much too stronger from any he's customary to know. Beware the Trappist monks! Our maroon Peugot 504 with sunroof was waiting in a fenced lot behind AutoZoom! on Pelikaanstraat. Guy at the front desk eyed Nils' papers warily before handing him the keys. We slammed the trunk and took off. Nils dodged streetcars, working his gearbox like a pro. The open road at last! Flying along Autoroute E10, wind hammering our faces. I accordioned his Michelin map; Europe flapped, whipped, threatened to shred. Squinting at threadlike red capillaries. Verdun! I hooted; an inch above Nancy. The Western Front. He shrugged; no problem making a scenic detour. I filled him with visions of 1916 as we sizzled south—twenty-ton Big Berthas belching thousand-pound shells, corpses rotting in trenches, cat-sized rats. Four hundred thousand dead in ten months, twice that many wounded or gassed. He was impressed; nothing this exciting happens in Danish army when he's making his two years required service. Signs for Waterloo flew by after Bruxelles. Charleroi, Philippeville. The farmland we cleaved—shaggy docktailed horses, cows chewing cuds in fluffed dandelion meadows—began to smell heartrendingly French. Guys in de Gaulle hats made us get out at the border, pop the trunk. A pair of German shepherds sniffed my Mouse and looked bored. N5 winding up through the Ardennes became N43 to Charleville-Mezieres; I wrapped my tongue around place names—flaking rust off the accent, suddenly aching for Paris. Stacked signs at crossroads pointed us towards Verdun. The town itself had a grey cathedral planted next to a limpid polleny river, several video stores trumpeting Macaulay Caulkin—hands clapped to ears, open-mouthed scream—in *Home Alone*. We followed official markers up gentle switchbacks. Nils slowed as we entered the forest. The Peugeot's engine ricocheted off overhanging trees, buzzing angrily. First clearing we came to held the Ossuaire; thousand of identical white crosses rowed neatly on mowed lawn, white marble mausoleum shaped like a surfaced submarine. A bronze plaque signed by Kohl and Mitterrand swore this tragedy would never be forgotten or repeated. We took off. I made Nils pull over when I saw the Boyau de Londres sign next to the remains of a trench snaking into a stand of roadside pines. Eighteen inches deep, lined with reinforced concrete stanchions, crumbling and rusted. Buttercups dotting both banks. I padded over, stepped in, crouched. You could almost imagine. Chalky white pebbles underfoot. Tracing a dry streambed back to the source. Fifty feet and the trail grew weed-choked, stanchions tilting like rotten teeth. I stood at the gloomy threshold, panting. Might as well piss, so I whipped it out. An animal cleared its throat behind clumped underbrush ten feet away. I whirled, repacked, and levitated back along the trench—tripping, flailing, scrambling. Go! I yelled. GO!! Nils popped open the door; I hurtled over the top, leaped and slammed. No trace of tusks or bristles when I turned to look but he left rubber anyway, flogging the gears.

Ten minutes later we were checking into a downtown hotel. Madame smiled when I mentioned my encounter. If monsieur will follow me, she said. She pointed at a wild boar's head over the fireplace. The mottled ivory prongs hurt to look at. He is a sanglier, monsieur. A bloodier. Such a nuisance! Always rooting around in our forest, digging up bones of the dead.

I caught up with my journal on the train to Paris Tuesday morning. Three hours was about right. The second cup of express helped me push through early cramping. Champagne country streamed by, rolling hills speckled with clumped vines, a triumph of agricultural organization. The two volumes clapped together when I finished felt heavy and earned. Paris! I lashed everything tightly and hauled my pack into the space between cars as we rattled through clothesline-draped suburbs. My Mouse made a good footrest. We hissed, squealed, slowed to a firm stop. Gare de l'Est was bustling and had the familiar Parisian smell, finely-chopped Gauloise smoke mixed with four-cylinder exhaust. I paused at quai-end to cinch my belt; three or four sparrows descended on our train's front bumper and began pecking at freshly-smashed bugs.

Paris was lyric under early-July skies, a sundress slipping off bare shoulders. The gypsy-woman had been alerted to my arrival and paid in advance; the note on my bed said Le Mazet at seven. Paul had tossed his toilet kit in the bidet. I kicked my stuff in a corner and flew downstairs, daypack bouncing. Boulevard Saint Michel was a familiar sloping glide past chestnut-shaded cafes. I fell into a wicker chair at Select Latin and ordered a creme. Women trotted by, braless as ever.

A young writer deserved this on his first day back. Tomorrow you'd be high over the Atlantic trying to convince yourself that the summer really happened. Truth is the remembered mingling of details and velocity. I flipped open my journal, squinted at embossed labeling on a nearby chair: J. Gatti, Rue Georges Pitard, 8, VAUgirard 63-84 PARIS XVieme. Twined brown, white, and maroon plastic caning. Tight as a tennis racket.

The waiter swung into view and set me up, tearing the receipt halfway after I'd settled. Velvety Italian cappuccino spoils you for French roast. I kept adding scalded milk, watching the mix lighten to the color of Rikki's palms until nothing was left. I snapped my journal shut, ducked down into the Metro. The rancid-dogshit smell of oxidized rubber wheels on track-level was weirdly comforting. Doors hissed open and shut. I fingered my ticket as we glided through tunnels, swaying on rusty sea legs. You learned to sing in this city. Chatelet/Les Halles had a sleepy siesta feel when we pulled in, leavened by distant drums. Four Andean Indians were working the top of the lower escalator; I dropped change in their ukulele case, next to a stack of silvery CDs. Pneumatic exit gates sucked in my ticket, parted, spit it out on the far side. I flew off the upper escalator into the glorious afternoon. Rainbow-tinged mist billowing off the fountain; hurdy-gurdy tinkling out of a carousel. No ball-and-chain of a Mouse! I flowed towards Boulevard de Sebastopol and across, past WHAAM! t-shirts—comic-strip fighter pilot blowing his antagonist out of the sky—with the Beaubourg looming suddenly, great gridded monolith presiding over sloping cobblestoned flats. Caricaturists lounging in directors' chairs down near the front doors. I stood at the crest. We always returned to Paris, no matter who we were or how it was changed or with what difficulties, or ease, it could be reached.

Lunch was a Heineken and sandwich grec avec frites wolfed down under a chestnut tree next to the beige pillbox porta-toilet at the top of the Plateau Beaubourg. A bearded hippie staggered up and pissed heavily against the side of the thing, groaning in satisfaction. A small mustachioed man with fierce eyes was preaching some sort of separatist program—Basque? Tunisian?—off a milk crate just behind me, accompanying himself on lute when bursts of song were required. An Asian woman in black tights at mid-plaza was dancing slowly into a huge plastic bag, cocooning, reemerging like a flown moth. *Swan Lake* pouring out of her boombox; a circle of onlookers at twenty paces.

I saw Finney and Babouche before they saw me. I'd just killed my beer and jumped up; they were bouncing past FastBurger—two skinny street kids sharing a bottle of wine, cackling. Then Babouche caught my eye and I had no chance to pretend I didn't see. You could hear his yell for blocks. Finney's hair was tied back and he'd gotten a tan. Hawaiian shirt exploding with flowers, leather sandals. My arm had barely recovered from Babouche's onslaught before Finney started pumping it, grinning. Heard about my rampage down south. Worked Nice last week himself, till his Strat was nicked. Shrugging, nodding at the acoustic guitar slung across his back. Been getting into a bit of singing lately. Nothing to write home about but the hippies seem to like it. Keeping out of trouble, mainly. Of course he's still crazy. Flics don't give you much chance to be anything else.

He didn't seem to remember we'd ever had a problem. Babouche sneered when I asked about Jorg. Reached into his dirty blond dreadlocks, pulled out a strip of razored steel taped for good gripping. Next time this guy is fucking with me? Pfffft.

The wine was five-franc red and warmed me all the way down. We made a small gleeful mob, chattering back past WHAAM! Finney wondered about my missing bottling hat, gave a thumbs-up when I explained about Rikki. Babouche nabbed an Orangina cup out of the trash.

We had our choice of cafes. I shoved harps in my cutoffs like derringers. A warm breeze kissed my thighs as we swung into position before a half-filled terrace. Finney's groove was the same but looser, freer; I locked in and held, balancing on my feet. None of our listeners seemed excited but nobody shooed us away either. Several older women smiled indulgently when Babouche came after them with his cup. We made out well, judging from the clinks. Finney's voice was as heartfelt as mine had ever been. We doubled up on the chorus of "Sweet Home Chicago." Twenty minutes of work bought us two more bottles of wine around the corner. My summer vacation suddenly seemed much too short. But I could live with this.

Paul was waiting at Le Mazet with the news that I was a star. We bear-hugged, slapped backs, old pros at this Europe game. Amsterdam he would tell me about momentarily. Veneration of sacred objects came first: freshly-minted copies of *The Muskegon Quarterly* and *The Berkeley Review* which he could not have been more surprised to find on the New Arrivals table at Shakespeare & Co. Voila.

I stared at my name on both covers; flipped open, riffled through. The prose—degree-zero style—was ruthlessly spare and devoid of poetry. Infidelities and nuclear anxieties. Hemingway and Kerouac the way a humorless young literary journalist would misread them. Somebody needed to get that guy shitfaced. Thank God for Billy Lee Grant.

We ended up at a table in back, under a mural: Renaissance troubadour with lute serenading a bonneted lass. Below that was the sign listing various cocktails de bieres. The waiter who brought our Kronenbourgs stood with pained resignation as I picked through my small hoard of change. Jammers at the next table—guitar, kazoo, spoons—were getting happy on "Sympathy for the Devil."

We clinked, Paul grimaced: And I thought *I* was the avatar of willful, sustained debauchery? Getting plastered on freebie drafts after the Heineken factory tour was the beginning of his downfall. So much for being alone in a strange city with nobody else's sanity to worry about. Did I know that the word "assassin" was derived from the hashish smoked by Arab gunmen to derange their senses? God rue the night he ingested Space Cake at the Melk Weg disco. He vaguely remembers wandering past funhouse mirrors into a darkened room where two women with shaved heads were anointing a large python with blue paint and proclaiming the birth of a New Lesbian Sisterhood before an audience of obscurely gendered social misfits who seemed happy for the snake. Call him old-fashioned; maybe none of this actually happened. Delusional psychosis does exist. Never again will he complain about being boring. Oh for the peaceful sanctity of Butler Library! Columbia here we come.

Before he forgot: he'd written a poem about Judith on the train down. Not that he was in any position to advise me about love. What were blues but the songs you salvaged from the wreckage of your battered heart? There were worse things to bring home from summer vacation than new poems. This one was for me, in any case. Cheers.

Hey Muse!

I am tired of writing poems
about women who leave me.
I am tired of turning frantic shock
into perfumed images,

tired of pretending
I can make something redeeming
out of wrenched guts
when all I really want to do

is sit alone in a dark room
howling
like a just-kicked dog.
My friends tell me, Never mind.

The other guy may get the girl;
you get the laurel leaf.
How much fun is that on a Saturday night?

Hey, Muse! Tell the Fates
that everyone down here
is bored with my constant aching.
Do me a favor:

Send me something new
to skip my pen to!

Paul Goldberg
July 198-
Amsterdam-Paris

Adam Gussow is an associate professor of English and Southern Studies at the University of Mississippi and a professional blues harmonica player and teacher. He is the author of three books on the blues, including *Mister Satan's Apprentice: A Blues Memoir*, the story of his experience as a Harlem street musician.